Look what people are saying about these authors....

Julie Kenner

Julie is known for her "flair for dialogue and eccentric characterizations."
—*Publishers Weekly*

"Funny and sassy, her books are a cherished delight."
—*Sherrilyn Kenyon*

"Kenner has a way with dialogue; her one-liners are funny and fresh. Her comic timing is beautiful, almost Jennifer Crusie-esque."
—*All About Romance*

Kathleen O'Reilly

"Kathleen O'Reilly's ability to write steamy, moving love stories leaves me breathless. I wouldn't miss one of her stories for love or money."
—*New York Times* bestselling author Julia London

"Romance is alive and doing just fine, thank you, in the capable hands of Kathleen O'Reilly."
—*The Romance Reader*

"If you rearrange the letters in 'Kathleen O'Reilly' it spells 'AUTO BUY.' Also, amazingly, 'REALLY GOOD BOOKS.'"
—Sarah, *TrashyBooks.com*

ABOUT THE AUTHORS

National bestselling author **Julie Kenner**'s first book hit the stores in February 2000, and she's been on the go ever since. Julie's books have been on lists as varied as those of *USA TODAY*, Waldenbooks, Barnes & Noble and *Locus* magazine. Julie lives in Georgetown, Texas, with her husband, two daughters and several cats.

Kathleen O'Reilly wrote her first romance at the age of eleven, which to her undying embarrassment was read aloud to her class. After taking more than twenty years to recover from the profound distress, she is proud to finally announce her career—romance author. Now she is an award-winning author of nearly twenty romances published in countries all over the world. Kathleen lives in New York with her husband and their two children, who outwit her daily.

Julie Kenner
Kathleen O'Reilly

JUST FOOLING AROUND

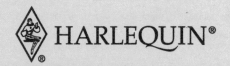

TORONTO • NEW YORK • LONDON
AMSTERDAM • PARIS • SYDNEY • HAMBURG
STOCKHOLM • ATHENS • TOKYO • MILAN • MADRID
PRAGUE • WARSAW • BUDAPEST • AUCKLAND

ISBN-13: 978-0-373-79535-2

JUST FOOLING AROUND
Copyright © 2010 by Harlequin Books S.A.

The publisher acknowledges the copyright holders of the individual works as follows:

CAM'S CATASTROPHE
Copyright © 2010 by Kathleen Panov

DARCY'S DARK DAY
Copyright © 2010 by Julia Beck Kenner

DEVON'S DILEMMA
Copyright © 2010 by Kathleen Panov

REG'S RESCUE
Copyright © 2010 by Julia Beck Kenner

Recycling programs
for this product may
not exist in your area.

CONTENTS

CAM'S CATASTROPHE
Kathleen O'Reilly

To Brenda, for a decade…and more to come!

Prologue

April 1, 1980

THE WORLD HAD NEVER SEEN four such dejected children. It was the evening of April Fools' Day, normally a time for hoaxes and pranks, but for the Franklin family, it was a dark day indeed. The full moon glowed with an eerie orange light, casting shadows on the barren midwestern farm and the small garden of gravestones, one newly dug.

Even the animals were smart enough to stay away when the events of April Fools' began to unfold. The cows watched warily from the far side of the pasture; owls hooted nervously, waiting for midnight to pass.

In the distance, the lights from the old farmhouse were all out, except for the last remaining guttering sparks of a kitchen fire nearly extinguished. Mother and Father Franklin were safe in their bed, pretending the day had passed without incident. It was only the children who were still awake, counting the ticks of the clock to midnight, counting the moments when their world passed from disaster back to normal once again.

The oldest boy, Cam, kicked at the marble gravestone, choosing to defy the fates, as was his way. His eye was blackened from a spirited encounter earlier in the day. At school, Leo Meeks, a larger and older student, had the spineless audacity to taunt Cam about the legend of the Franklin Curse, never an easy subject with any of the Franklin children. Cam, choosing to ignore the school principal's stern warning, had lit into the bully, but had discounted the newly waxed floors. So instead of ramming his fist into Leo's meaty face, he had instead rammed his own face into the nearest bank of lockers.

"She should have told us," he demanded of absolutely no one in particular, proceeding to kick at the stone until his foot began to ache. "She should have told somebody before she died. We can beat this. We just need to know how."

The eldest daughter, Devon, popped up from behind the lightning-split elm tree, a position she had chosen because it was statistically unlikely that lightning would strike twice in the same place. The tree also provided an excellent vantage point. "You heard Mom. Grandmother was batty as a fruitcake. There's no way to beat it, Cam. You and Reg are wasting your time."

The youngest child, Darcy, dug her hand in the grass, and happily picked out a four-leaf clover. "Look! It's a lucky clover. I think it's a sign from Grandmother that we're not cursed after all."

Devon looked at the clover and scoffed, "That's a weed."

Darcy first sniffed then folded the clover in her pocket. "It's a pretty weed, and I think Grandmother would want us to keep it…even if she was batty."

Reg, who was the most scholarly of the four, shook

his head, his keen gaze scanning the night skies as if the answers were in the stars. "She wasn't that batty. She said it started in the eighteenth century, with Olivia d'Espry, but she doesn't know the story—she doesn't know why. That's what I want to find out."

Cam muttered something vaguely scatological in disagreement, because he sensed manure when he heard it. "It's just a story," he muttered.

"The pieces fit," Reg countered. "Olivia came from France to New Orleans with her father. Our family tree cuts through New Orleans, too."

"And that's when Great-grandpa Franklin first wrote about the curse," Devon said. "Or great-great. Or something. Anyway, back when he was in New Orleans."

"Archives don't lie," Reg said. "History doesn't lie. It makes sense."

"The hell it does," Cam said. "It is what it is."

"It will make sense," Reg said. "I'm going to figure it out. I'm going to stop it."

They all looked at him, not believing, but then Reg's watch alarm began to chirp. Midnight.

Another day had passed. Another year's reprieve. Another year to hope.

1

"I DON'T CARE what the bone-headed insurance company is telling you. That's my social-security number, there are no inverted digits and I didn't steal it."

Safe on the other side of the E.R. ward, Dr. Jenna Ferrar watched the scene unfold, and shook her head in chagrin. Cameron Franklin's belligerent tone would get him nowhere with Bertrice, the guardian of hospital registrations, a woman secretly known as Ballbuster Bertie. After four years of this, you'd think he would know better. Apparently not.

Still, Jenna didn't understand how Bertie could get mad at somebody with a cast on his arm, and those deep, honey-brown eyes that had the ability to snuff out a woman's virginity with one smoldering glance.

Every year on April Fools' Day, he was in her E.R. with something new. Last year it was a broken leg sustained while hang gliding. The year before, it was a motorcross accident, complete with a distal radius fracture and more lacerations than Alfred Hitchcock could ever imagine.

Even with all the medical trauma, she still wanted to

pull him behind the curtain and show him how doctor was meant to be played.

What she couldn't figure out was why Bertie was immune. Every other female in the E.R. had spent many a private moment in the staff lounge, fantasizing about Cam Franklin—including Jenna.

Paging Doctor McSlutty…

Feeling the familiar pangs, her medically trained scrutiny drifted over his anatomy in a purely nonprofessional manner.

The sling on his arm did nothing to detract from the finely tapered torso, the shaggy mane of sun-streaked brown hair and the ass that…well, in her line of work there were few backsides she wanted to see nude. But *his*…two bulbous cheeks lovingly gift-wrapped in faded Levi's…da Vinci couldn't have sketched it any better.

Discreetly, she raised a hand and fanned her own flushed cheeks.

Three years ago, she'd almost invented a tetanus scare in order to ask him to drop his trousers. In the end, she chickened out—pesky medical ethics and potential for malpractice. But even knowing those risks, the temptation had been strong.

Seeing there was no hope for gratuitous nudity this year, either, she stuffed her hands into the pockets of her lab coat and watched Bertie and Cam argue with ever-increasing wrath.

Before she could intervene, her cell phone beeped. It was her sister.

"What?" she answered, her eyes still focused on Cam, thinking that no man should look that sexy when he was irate and medicated.

"Are you okay?" asked Janie.

"Why?"

"Your voice sounds goofy. A little wobbly. Why is it wobbly?"

Jenna cleared her throat, erasing some of the lust, which was always a problem when Cam was around. "Better?"

"Ah, yes. Now there's the crisp, no-nonsense sister I know and love. I need a favor."

"No, I will not go out with Tony's business partner," she insisted, hoping to get off the phone soon. The patients were starting to notice the argument at the desk, and Larry the Security Guard had already peeped over there twice.

"No fix-ups. That wasn't the favor. Can you talk to Mom?"

"Why can't you do it?"

"You're the doctor."

"You're the mother, the wife, the managing director of a billion-dollar foundation. That's not peanuts. That should count."

"I'm afraid of her."

"I'm afraid of her, too. It's why we're hardened and driven and overcompensate in all other areas of achievement. In many ways, that very terror is responsible for our success. Embrace your fears. Call her yourself."

"She wants me to come to San Diego with her. To a spa." Janie dragged out the words like a death sentence.

"Go. Sounds like fun."

"You're not listening to me, are you? Because if you were really listening, you would have expressed the appropriate levels of shock and horror at the idea of spending a weekend with Mother. A weekend that involves mud and creepy levels of nakedness. It could scar me for life."

"You are scarred for life, get over it." Tough love was the motto in the Ferrar family, except when it came to men. Then they were mush. Jenna cast a mush-filled look at Cam and sighed.

"You won't go? You could go. I'll tell her that you should go."

"I'm needed here. I have to save lives."

"That's a likely story."

She noticed that Bertie seemed ready to kill. Not so unlikely. "Can't go."

"I hate you."

"No you don't."

"I could hate you."

"No you won't. Who would go shopping with you and tell you that fleece sweatpants are actually flattering and you don't need to feel guilt for dressing like a frump? No one, because the people that love you are the ones that will lie."

"You're going to make me go?"

"Grow a pair. Tell her no," encouraged Jenna, who had lusted after Cam Franklin for four years, and had done exactly nothing. Yes, there was irony. Janie would never know.

"I can't tell her no, she's my mother," pleaded Janie, but Jenna heard the resignation in her voice.

"Hanging up now, sis."

"Noo…."

Jenna ended the call and started toward the reception desk, thinking that maybe it was time for her to grow a pair, as well.

"You don't need to call the police. There is no crime," Cam was saying, almost a bellow, but not quite. Safely behind the bulletproof glass partition, Bertie jumped up and glared, eyes promising death. "If you don't back away from my window, there will be crime, mister."

Cam leaned forward and pressed his nose to the glass. "Try me, you little pencil-pushing gnome."

Uh-oh. Name-calling. Not good.

Briskly Jenna moved through the crowd of four sniffling sneezers, two achy backs, eight cases of dental malaise and one tiny tot, currently running a temp of 99.3. All in all, it was a relatively quiet Thursday night for Manhattan—except for World War III at the Admissions window.

"Bertie? Is there a problem?"

"Is an asshole considered a problem, Dr. Ferrar? I think not. I consider it an official hazard of duty, and if this patient thinks he can pull a fast one on Bertie, he can think again."

The patient in question—Cameron Franklin, age thirty two, one hundred and eighty-three pounds, unmarried, employed by King, Franklin and Cross Development, O positive blood type and no communicable diseases—turned toward her and, as usual, Jenna had to stifle her sudden case of labored breathing. Those tiger-bright eyes always made her squirm.

"Can you make her practice reason and logic? Do we have to take the word of some mindless, faceless, corporate bureaucrat over what? Five years of actual hospital history? My social-security number has not changed. It's the same one I was born with, the same one I had last year. The same one you wrote in your paperwork the year before, and the year before that. If you love the records so much, look at your own paperwork."

That last bit was directed at Bertrice, who for the first time in twenty years on the job, actually looked uncertain. She stared down at the manila folder in front of her, thumbed through a few pages and frowned. Then, she picked up the next folder, thumbed through a few more pages and scowled. Finally she looked up at Cam, sulky and unhappy, like a two-year-old missing her favorite toy. "I think the records are wrong," she mumbled.

Jenna knew that Cam would pick up on the half-hearted tone. He did.

"All of them? Even the ones that you wrote? Last year? And the year before? No way. There is no freaking way that you could make a mistake," he told Bertie, voice dripping with sarcasm.

"I don't make mistakes," Bertie defended. It was true. Although lacking in her customer-service skills, Bertie was meticulous. However, sometimes, the unthinkable could happen.

Jenna coughed discreetly. "Bertrice. Normally I wouldn't dare correct you, but I think that's his correct social-security number."

"See? If Doc Ferrar believes me, don't you think you should?"

Cam beamed, those kissably full lips curving upwards. Jenna, who was more driven by token gold-star signs of approval than she cared to admit, beamed back.

Bertrice picked up the pile of folders and raised her brows. "I don't think I should. But I will. This is gonna take a while to fix, and if you think I'm going to hurry, well, mister, I'm going to make me a new definition for slow. In fact, I'm going to be so slow, they're going to put me in the dictionary right next to the turtles. And don't go anywhere, neither. 'Cause we know where you live and I'll hunt you down."

After Bertrice left, Cam turned to Jenna and dragged his hand through his thick hair, tousling it. Not surprisingly, it made him look even more bedable.

"I thought a hospital was a place for mercy and charity, a patient-centered haven nurturing the physical well-being of the wounded and infirm."

"Nah. You've got us confused with those hospitals on TV. In real life, it's all about preventative care. If the customer service is hell, maybe people will stay away. We keep hoping, but no such luck. Speaking of ineffective diagnosis, what are you in for this year?"

"Parkour."

"What is parkour? It sounds exotic and slightly poisonous."

"It's running. Well, running on an industrialized path, and you jump and climb over stuff. Very stylized."

"You do this in the city?" she asked, thinking it was a miracle no taxi had smashed him flat.

"Oh, yeah. Construction sites are actually the best."

"And that's how you got hurt?"

"Sort of. I was doing this monkey vault on some scaffolding for one of our buildings, jumping from one cross-brace to another, followed by a flawless underbar through the top-level beam and then ending with a cat leap to the top of this old warehouse next door. It was great, everybody should try this, the wind rushing through your ears, like you're flying, but right when I was reaching for the brick on the warehouse, this goose decided to dive-bomb me and I lost my focus, and the rest can be found in my X rays. Dislocated shoulder."

It was apparent he loved what he did, but sometimes his eyes gleamed a little too bright, were a little too focused. It was then when Jenna worried.

"Cam, one of these days, you're going to kill yourself."

Sadly, he didn't even look concerned. "Then that's one less patient you'll have to treat."

"I'd rather up my stats the old-fashioned way, instead of being Dr. Death Angel. And by the way, you could help out by staying home on April Fools'."

He met her eyes, serious, intent. "So you believe the curse is true?"

It was a discussion they'd had every year and every year, she was just as uncomfortable. However, she knew enough to keep her impassive-doctor face in place. "It doesn't matter whether it exists or not. Even without a curse, you'd still end up in my E.R. on April One because you have to be all Mr. Stupid-Head. It'd be flattering to think this is all an elaborate and painful ruse to get my attention, but I don't think it is."

Damn it.

"If I wanted to get your attention, you'd know," he told her, flashing her a smile that indicated he had some ideas. Possibly involving the loss of clothing. Instantly her blood pressure spiked, and Jenna worked to remember who she was. A doctor. Professional. Detached. Capable of coherent speech no matter what sort of debauched images were rolling around in her head.

"Cam, next year, stay home."

"I'm not going to let it beat me," he said, the smile disappearing from his face.

Jenna stared pointedly at the sling on his arm. "It's already beat you."

Before he could argue more, her pager beeped, and she shot him a long, frustrated look, because all of her brilliant advice was passing straight through that stubborn head.

Some of her concern must have seeped through, because then Cam leaned over to kiss her cheek, a patronizing yet still sweet gesture. However, Jenna was no fool.

She twisted and found herself mouth to mouth—exactly as she intended. His lips moved over hers, warm, persuasive, instantly morphing from surprise to seduction with an ease that spoke of an ego-shattering amount of practice. His fingers lifted to her throat, an oddly intimate touch that stoked her more than most of her sexual experiences.

When he pulled away, she was pleased to see the dilated pupils, the shallow breathing. Exactly as she intended.

Now, she told herself, *say something provocative and sexy.* However, Doctor McSlutty was nowhere in the building.

Her pager beeped again, and he waved his good hand. "See you next year."

They were the cocky and dismissive words of a fool, and Jenna fisted her hands in her coat before she hit something—or someone.

"No," she snapped, ignoring the curious looks of the staff. It wasn't often she lost it with a patient, but so what? She was human. Mostly.

"I don't want to see you next year," she lectured in her best I-Am-God voice. "Be a stranger."

At first she thought her words were falling on deaf ears, and she turned to walk away. However, she could feel the heat of his eyes on her, thinking, considering. It probably wouldn't make a bit of difference, but at least she'd tried.

Tried? That wasn't trying. If she really wanted to make a difference, she needed to do something more. Something risky. Something daring. Something she'd always wanted to do.

Then, while her stomach was still convulsing with the aftereffects of sexual palpitations, Dr. Jenna Ferrar got a bold and slightly idiotic idea.

She'd have to wait three hundred and sixty-four days before implementation, but some things were worth waiting for.

Her fingers brushed over her lips, still feeling the heat. Yes. It was definitely idiotic, but even worse, three hundred and sixty-four-days was a long, long time away…

2

March 31: 364 days later

IT WAS ABOUT TIME. Cam watched as the steel girders were hoisted into the blue skies and smiled with satisfaction as he always did at the start of a new site.

Sure, the building wasn't going to be a New York City landmark, but it would be a perfect low-rent apartment complex that was sorely needed. Time to call it a day, because there was lots to do before tomorrow. After he checked in with the foreman, he packed up the plans and was headed toward the subway when one of the crew called after him.

"Hey, Cam. Try and come back in one piece this time."

Cam grinned, holding up his middle finger, a symbol of so many things in his life. He never came back in one piece, but he always came back. All of the other Franklins feared the curse, but not Cam. Nope, he embraced it. He taunted it. Did anybody think that some ancient hoodoo was going to alter his lifestyle? No way in hell. Sure, his partners thought he was a bit light in the head, but Cam didn't mind. He'd rather be stupid than whipped. This way, by taunting the gods, he took the day on his terms.

Tomorrow was powerboat racing. Forty knots, the slap of the ocean spray on your face, and plumes of water that rose like a geyser. Cam looked up at the skyline, at the towering line of structures that didn't take shit from anyone or anything.

It was why he'd chosen civil engineering. Building things, defying gravity, man over anything that got in his way.

The way it was meant it to be.

In short order, the crowded and ever-efficient New York subway system had him back at his apartment, washing the day's grime from his skin.

The boat race was out on Long Island, far away from the city, and he was going to miss the annual walk of shame into the St. Catherine's E.R. Actually, he was going to miss Dr. Jenna Ferrar, with that long, dark hair, those sexy Dr. Dominatrix eyes, and the lean, tight curves that even a lab coat couldn't hide.

Just the memory of her—actually, it was more the memory of a naked her—made him painfully hard, and because he conveniently happened to be in the shower, he took matters into his own hand, capping off the day, and exorcising her memory all in one fell swoop.

A thousand times he'd nearly trekked in on his own, merely to see if she was there, see if she wanted to get a cup of coffee, see if she wanted to come home with him, but he always left it alone.

There were women he dated, women he slept with, women he took to a club, but they all ended up three dates and out. In his heart, Cam knew that one day he wasn't going to come home in one piece. You could only cross fate so often, but damn it, he wasn't going to play a victim, either. Hiding out like his sister Devon? Letting the tension eat at him like a disease. Not in this lifetime.

Cam was clean, packed and ready to sit down with a cold beer when the buzzer rang. Immediately he glanced at his watch, but 8:00 p.m. was too early for the really crap stuff to start. It was four hours to midnight, four hours before hell night began.

The bell ringer was probably some lost salesman, or a package for a neighbor. Curious, he punched the call button.

"Got a visitor, Mr. Franklin. She says to tell you it's Jenna. Personally, I would advise you to let her up, sir, even if you don't know her, if you know what I mean."

Jenna? He only knew one Jenna. The doc. Here?

Whoa.

His eyes scanned the apartment for female unsuitables. Finding none, he snagged a shirt from the closet and shrugged into it, buttoning it up to something approaching nonslob.

He pressed the call button. "Send her up, Carlton."

"Good luck, Mr. Franklin. You should know I'm a very jealous man."

March 31, 8:00 p.m.

JENNA'S HEART was beating somewhere that was anatomically impossible when Cam opened the door. It was strange to see him without a cast, or brace, or pale from loss of blood.

Tonight, he looked hale, hearty, able to fulfill her every fantasy, which for Jenna was quite extensive. The demands of the medical profession didn't allow much in the way of a satisfactory sex life. A date here, a quickie there (usually regretted) and long nights alone with her romance novels and other electronic accoutrements to aid in keeping her de-stressed.

Her stress levels began to rise, mainly due to the way he stared at her. His dark eyes tracing over her with an X-ray vision that could see through her Burberry trench coat, see through her attractive and cleavage-augmenting red dress, see through the brand-new black demi-bra and matching panty, see straight through to her nipples, which were currently jutting out like twin torpedoes. It was a perfectly natural reaction, she reminded herself—a scientific justification that did absolutely no good in easing her awkwardness.

He looked at her, curiously, appreciatively. "I rate house calls?"

"It's not a house call," she answered. It was almost the truth. "I knew you'd be in tomorrow and I thought I'd get all the paperwork out of the way first. You know, avoid any problems that might arise."

At the feeble, somewhat porno-sounding premise, his eyes gleamed, seeming to say, "I know why you're here." It was not a comfortable moment for a woman who had won the Mayers-Andrews Fellowship, not that she expected anything different. In fact, she reminded herself, it was exactly the animalistic reaction she had planned on, which soothed her ego but did nothing to ease the nipple-peak.

Down, girls.

"Come on in," he invited, like the spider to the fly. Of course, that would mean that he was the fly, because this was her plan, so why didn't she feel like the spider? No, she definitely felt like the fly.

Yeesh, she was rambling. In a completely fly-like move, she wrapped her arms across her chest, above the nips, above the bra, above the dress, above the trench coat.

It didn't help.

Quickly she scurried into his apartment. "I can't stay very long," she told him with a nervous smile, flicking her hair back, wondering if he'd noticed that she had the ends trimmed.

Don't think about the hair, she thought. *Don't think about the man.* Instead she focused on the array of sporting equipment that lined the wall. There were baseball bats, an assortment of balls, a tennis racket and bag of golf clubs, but no pads or helmets. In fact, there were no safety devices at all.

"Quite the athlete."

"I have some excess energy. It helps." He moistened his lips, and she caught the movement, her eyes drawn, glued, until she blinked her vision free.

"Would you like a drink?" he offered politely, walking into the small kitchen that was off the main room, leaving her alone.

"Water, please," she called, thinking that sobriety might be a good thing.

"I have wine," he said, poking his head back into the room. "A few years ago, I went ballooning in Napa. The vineyards felt bad after the accident, so they sent me a few cases. It's really good stuff."

"I'll take it."

"You can take off your coat," he yelled from the kitchen. A perfectly courteous remark that did not mean strip. Still, Jenna hesitated, then told herself she was being way too prudish for someone who had prepared a *whole year* for this grand seduction.

Quickly she slid the trench coat off, adjusted her boobs, straightened her dress, sat on the couch and crossed her legs in her most attractive pose.

When Cam reentered the room, he paused, taking in the legs, the dress, the boobs. The pause grew longer, and Jenna noted the pronounced swelling beneath his jeans, indicating growing sexual arousal. A small sound emerged from her throat. In layman's terms, they called it a moan.

Okay, the plan was working.

In his hands were two glasses and a bottle of cabernet. An entire bottle was good. It said, *Linger, kick back, let me climb underneath your clothes.*

"Wow, you look very nice without a lab coat. Your dress, I mean. Very attractive."

"It's just something I—" *picked out four months ago* "—threw on." She lifted the glass to her lips, gulped, feeling the warmth of the alcohol being absorbed in her blood. Actually, it was medically impossible for the lightheadedness and fever to be caused by alcohol, not this fast. But she blamed it on the drink anyway.

"You have the paperwork?" he asked, seemingly not affected by the alcohol at all.

Jenna licked her lips and he noticed. She leaned over to get the forms from her purse, and her neckline gaped, possibly exposing a hint of black lace that she hadn't planned on exposing this early, but he noticed, and she noticed that he noticed.

She fumbled in her purse, digging past the condoms,

lotions and handcuffs, until her fingers clasped the papers. Hands trembling, she pushed them toward him.

"You seem nervous," he stated, a completely obvious statement that didn't need to be put out there for public consumption. Jenna had been a National Merit Scholar, scored 10.3 on the MAC and won a prestigious (somewhat) prize for medical service. In light of her other accomplishments, did she have to be a genius at seduction, as well? *No.*

"I think I have the beginnings of a cold. Chills. Fever." She sniffed. "Congestion."

"Sorry."

"It'll pass."

"Do you want me to fill these out?" he asked her, glancing at the papers.

"I think it would be more efficient, don't you?"

"Actually, you made the trip for nothing. I'm not going to be in the city tomorrow. The boat race is way out, the tip of Long Island. It's about four hours from here."

Completely oblivious to how easily he had decimated her plans, Cam handed the papers back to her, an artless smile playing on his lips.

Bastard.

So now what, genius?

"Have you checked out the hospitals in the area? Southampton has a good trauma unit. Most boat injuries are head injuries or drownings. Have you considered that you might get chopped up in a propeller?"

Undaunted, he clicked her glass. "To not getting chopped up in a propeller."

Normally, her patients nodded and wrote down her instructions, word for word. People did not argue with their doctors. They did not disagree with them, or doubt their ability to know all. Except for Cam.

It was time for a more direct approach. Pleading, in fact.

"Cam, don't go."

He pushed a hand through the thick thatch of hair, exposing a tense jaw, and angry eyes. Obviously he took his life risks seriously.

"That's why you're here? To talk me out of this?"

Jenna thought about denying it, but that would involve confessing deeper, darker secrets involving sexual motivations. No, copping to the easier answer seemed best.

"That was my first approach, yes."

"It won't work."

Yes, she was beginning to get that.

Boldly, she gulped down the last of the wine and conquered her nerves. She was thirty-one, not thirteen. He found her attractive—dare she say it, highly attractive. Gathering her courage, she inhaled deeply, breasts rubbing against cool silk and lace. It was erotic. It was liberating. Doctor Sugarpants was in.

"Then I'm on to Plan B," she said in a silky voice. Emboldened, she pulled the band from her hair, shaking it loose, and she noticed the way his hands bit into his thighs. Hard.

It was about time the patient respected the doc.

"What's Plan B?" he asked.

She shot him a half smile and coughed discreetly.

"Sex."

3

TAKING ADVANTAGE OF her momentary adrenaline rush, Jenna stripped her dress over her head and flung it on the other side of the couch. When she was finished, she braced her arm across the back of his couch and gave him a smoldering look, a *Penthouse* siren in black lace bra, panties and sheer black hose. There was no man alive who could resist her.

Across from her, Cam sat. Frozen. Resisting her.

Keep the adrenaline moving. Flowing. Ignore the icy chill. You're a siren. Be the siren. You play God on a daily basis. How hard can this be?

Still he sat.

In her highly overworked mind, this whole evening had gone much differently. For instance, in her version of how everything would play out, he would have ripped her clothes off immediately.

Where was the ripping?

"Don't you have anything to say?" she asked, and yes, there might been a quiver in her voice.

"I think I swallowed my tongue."

"Then it's very convenient that I'm a trained professional," she answered. Some of her nerves were starting to ease. Now they were talking. Now he was falling into line.

"Dr. Ferrar…" he started, and she held up a hand.

"Excuse me, but when a woman is in your living room in her underwear, it's best to drop the formalities."

"Jenna."

It pleased her to hear him say it. The way his voice got deep and rumbled in his throat.

"Yes?"

"I don't think this is a good idea."

"I know it's not a good idea, but it's the best one I have."

There was an odd look on his face, uncomfortable and annoyed. Finally, he spit it out. "I don't like being a mercy fuck."

Mercy fuck? Jenna could only stare. He had no idea how long she had worked with a personal trainer. The lengths she had gone to to find the exact perfect lingerie. Yes, she might be a doctor, committed to the caring and compassion, but compassion only went so far. As far as Jenna was concerned, there was compassion and then there was sex, and never the twain shall meet.

"There is no mercy involved." Except perhaps for that moment when he was pounding inside of her, and she was begging and pleading for mercy….

"I know what you're doing. You're trying to keep me here. It's flattering and really bighearted, but seriously, I'm not your personal mission."

Did he truly believe that, or was this some devious, underhanded way of subverting her authority and going about his own merry way, terrorizing emergency rooms everywhere?

Jenna studied the innocent gleam in his eye, and

decided that yes, this man was devious, underhanded and stubborn.

She chose her words carefully.

"Don't be so stupid. You are a man. A sexual being. If you sit there rejecting my advances, then I'll have no choice but to assume that either I'm repulsive or you're gay."

The innocent little twinkle faded, and he cupped his burgeoning crotch. "Not gay." She glared and he backtracked even further. "And you're not repulsive. Not even close."

"Glad to get that out of the way, but I'm a little out of my depth here. Yes, I'm willing to strip and portray myself as a woman of loose morals and yogalike flexibility. But for the record, it won't be pretty. It won't be graceful, but it would be heartfelt."

"I think it'd be real pretty," he murmured, a flattering bit of awe in his voice. It was about time he showed some appreciation for a naked, not repulsive woman in his living room.

"Cam…" she said, leaning forward with earnest sincerity and not in some slutty move to flash him her breasts.

The breast move worked. She could see that some of the determination faded, and when he spoke, he spoke to her cleavage. "Jenna, this is not smart."

"Smart? You will lecture me on smart? This from the man who mutilates his body on an annual basis? I'd say that the smartest move you could make was to—" she waved a fill-in-the-blank hand "—make a move."

Silently he stared, but she was winning, and now they both knew it. It was there in the furtive glances that dipped beyond her Pilates-flat belly, toward the front of the sheer, extraordinarily sheer, black lace panties.

Boldly she opened her legs, splayed them in a triple-X move that was designed to draw attention to her pelvic region.

His gaze locked there. Glazed. Almost Pavlovian. Fascinating.

"I'm still leaving in the morning," he stated firmly, ceding the battle but claiming the war.

As if.

Jenna smiled her sweetest, most innocent smile and stood. She reached behind her, trying to unhook her bra, but the clasp was stuck or maybe her fingers were swollen. Whatever the case, she couldn't undo the tiny eye hooks. Who the hell had designed this sucker? Master Lock?

Before she made a complete fool of herself, he turned her, and she felt his hands on her back. Some of the cold melted away. He had nice hands. Large, rough palms and long fingers that were destined to know the secret of the bra clasp.

But he didn't undo it right away. Instead, those big hands slid beneath the strap, stroking, caressing.

"What are you doing?"

"Touching you. I thought that was the idea. You're very touchable."

The long strokes continued, up and down, excruciatingly gentle. "I thought you were a builder," she murmured, tilting her head back, eyes closed, in imminent danger of losing all sense of balance.

"Yeah. So?"

"You don't have a builder's hands," she said, her breath escaping on a whisper.

"You don't have a doctor's breasts, but you don't see me ragging on you about it."

"What sort of breasts do I have?" she asked, swallowing when his hands moved up, curling around her shoulders, her neck. Not content, those hands slid down her front, slipping beneath the silken fabric of the bra, freeing her breasts.

"Soft to the touch, highly sensitive." His thumbs flicked over the twin nipples, toying them to attention, and Jenna felt her knees start to tremble. He pulled her closer, bracing her from shoulder to knee. She felt the bulky chest, the rough friction of his jeans against her bare skin, and the long piece of his cock that was pressing impatiently against her ass.

He continued the sure movements with his hands, a slow languid survey that was turning her to a boneless mass of tissue and nerves. It had been so long since she'd felt like this. Relaxed, pleasured…*healed.* Next his clever mouth explored the slope of her neck, finding an erotic little spot behind her ear that she didn't even know she had.

"There?" he asked.

"There is nice," she said on a sigh.

While his mouth dallied, his hands moved lower, beneath the band of the panties. "You don't have a doctor's underwear, either."

"You have a problem with that?" she asked, liking this teasing, liking the touch. He'd surprised her with this. Surprised her with his patience. It wasn't easy for her to relax; there was always something else on the list to be done. But right now, she only wanted to do this.

"I want you to lose them," he whispered, sliding the scrap of material down her legs, until it fell to the floor, leaving her bare except for hose and heels. Yes, it wasn't completely comfortable, but she was okay with that, because she was starting to feel…sexy.

His rough thumbs traced over her cheeks, parting the highly charged flesh, and making her hips tighten with his flirting touch. "So soft, so tempting. An ass this fine should not be covered."

"There are a lot of nerve endings there," she explained, not that he needed the anatomical education, but by talking, by keeping her mind focused on the logistics of what they were doing, she didn't feel quite so…*emotional.*

Not that emotional was a bad thing, but she did twelve-hour rotations with her feelings packed in ice. Letting go wasn't easy for her. Letting someone else take over wasn't in her nature.

In fact, her body jerked in protest, just from the feel of his hands. He cupped her cheeks, kneaded, and her body jerked again. Toward him. "It's a very sensitive area," she hissed, her eyes desperately locked to the view from his window. She wanted him to stop touching her, even while she could feel the moisture beading down her thigh. Her instinct was to turn to see, to watch, to know what to expect, but the complex sensations that were roiling inside her kept her frozen, nervous and highly aroused.

She heard a shuffling noise and felt him press his mouth to said sensitive nerve endings, and she shivered at the frankly wicked touch. Standing naked while a man kissed her ass hadn't been in her nature either… until now.

Then his hand slid between her legs, one long finger finding the heavy seam that frankly couldn't take much more. She heard his sigh and wondered how he could be so relaxed, when she was about to hit the ceiling. Her hands fisted, clenched, in a mirror move to the stroke of his hands. Every nerve, every muscle, every cell in her was tuned to the rhythm of that finger. Slyly he explored between her thighs, the vulva, expanding the labia majora, and then oh please yes…the labia minora.

"More. Nerve endings. There," she bit out, her muscles clenched because Cam was finding each and every sensory receptor, and did she know she could get this stimulated?

His mouth touched her, and her heart stopped.

"Cam…" she pleaded, because this wasn't her.

He took pity on her, and in one easy move, he lowered her to the couch and slid his big body over her, his eyes remarkably tender for a man who assaulted himself on an annual basis.

"The first time I saw you, I got embarrassingly hard, thinking of you…like this." He gaze raked over her, heavy-lidded and hungry, and instantly Jenna knew what was for dinner. Instead of being nervous, she felt tense and raw…excited.

"The first time you saw me, you had a concussion. Vision can be…compromised."

"There were two of you. Both of you were naked."

Then his mouth took hers, soft on her lips, and she could taste him, taste herself. His tongue slid between her lips, so slow, so insidious. Once again, there was that rhythm.

She loved the way he kissed, that easy slow glide of his tongue that lulled her like the ocean. Her bare hips rose higher, grinding against the thick bulge in his jeans, so close, yet so far…. He laughed, low and dastardly, and then thrust against her, denim to skin, and her eyes drifted closed. This time when his hands returned to her thighs, she was the one who sighed, arching her swollen breasts into the rough cotton of his shirt. Then his finger slid inside her again, and she laughed, trying for low and dastardly, as well. Instead, she sounded nervous.

For good reason.

His tongue licked her belly, the curve of her waist, and she sucked in a breath at the decadent contact, feeling an answering pulse of desire between her legs.

"Cam?"

"Yes," he whispered in between those magical kisses.

His hands parted her soft folds, and he pressed a hungry kiss there…in the clitorial region, where a large earthquake was starting to form.

Her hips arched up to meet that talented, tickling tongue.

"You don't…have a builder's…mouth," she told him, trying to keep her brain from exploding.

Cam lifted his head and smiled. "It's all engineering. Every component can only stand so much stress before it buckles."

And then he proceeded to demonstrate. The stroke of his tongue was longer, more liquid, or maybe that was her, but she could definitely feel the force of the orgasm building inside her. Each flick across her überjuiced flesh created a new tremor. Her heels dug into the couch, sliding back and forth. The ever-increasing pressure began to drive her to the breaking point.

"Cam," she warned, her hands grabbing the cotton of his shirt. She wanted skin, she wanted flesh. She wanted relief.

"Break for me," he ordered, and then he took her clit in his mouth and suckled her. Hard. The spasms began, her muscles primed for explosion.

It was too much. Jenna shattered.

4

CAM ROSE UP on his elbows and decided that he'd never seen anything so heart-stoppingly sexy in his entire life. Dr. Jenna Ferrar was splayed on his couch, her face flushed with satisfaction, long dark hair playing peeka-boo with the dusky nipples and long legs encased in sheer black hose. The gleaming evidence of her pleasure glistened on the swollen pink skin between her thighs.

Cam closed his eyes for a second, memorizing the image.

Until her brisk fingers started working the buttons on his shirt. "I don't understand why everything is so small."

He moved her hands aside, helping her. "It's a good thing you're not a surgeon."

"Oh, blow me, mister. Get the shirt off. Drop the trousers."

Not only capable, but bossy, as well. Happily, Cam obeyed, tossing his clothes aside, until he was flat over her.

However, he wouldn't let her lose the hose. "You can't," he said, when she would have taken them off. "I'm still living out fantasies I didn't even know I had."

She laughed and pulled his mouth down to hers. "How can you wake up in the morning and leave this?" she whispered against his lips, and he wanted to argue.

To tell her that this was a pleasant diversion, but that tomorrow he still had plans. However, then he felt that bossy tongue in his mouth, her legs wrapping around him, her hips grinding against him, back and forth, and there was no argument in the world that would have kept him from this.

"Inside me. Please," she urged, and she didn't have to say anything twice.

He sheathed his cock in a condom, pushed deep inside her and watched as her eyes turned wild. Damn, he loved to see that. The cool, composed doctor stripped bare, lying beneath him. He'd wanted her for so long.

Wanted this.

Jenna.

Tight. Wet. Surrounding him.

Each time he moved, her eyes flared open, so startled, so shocked, so...*good*.

She looked up at him, pouting breasts, her mouth open and moist. There was such a storm in her expressive dark eyes. Pure pleasure. Pure lust.

He kissed that mouth, his tongue thrusting inside her, his cock thrusting inside her. Her hands grabbed at his back, his ass, urging him on.

Cam began to move faster.

Her fingernails raked over his back; there would be marks, but he didn't mind. He lifted her hips higher, raising her up, losing himself in that hot, wet channel. As he listened to the slap of skin, the heavy gasps of much-needed air, he forgot about the boat race, forgot about his plans and just focused on this. On her.

"Come, Jenna."

"Faster. Need faster," she ordered.

Cam drove in harder, deeper, back and again, until his body felt like fire. He could feel the climax inside him, feel the juices waiting to flow, and he knew he couldn't last much longer. But still, he wanted her over, wanted her first, and he curved those pretty legs over his shoulders, staring straight into paradise, watching the joining of their bodies, watching her hips arch higher and higher.

The mantel clock struck midnight. April Fools'.

Cam could only smile.

JENNA WAS GOING to die. Cardiac arrest. She could feel the overtaxed organ pumping in time with Cam's powerful thrusts; her body wasn't going to survive. Desperate, she grabbed a fistful of couch and held on tight, trying to breathe, trying to scream.

She could see him watching her. See the determination in his face, the sheen of sweat that slicked his hair, his chest.

Oh, yes.

This wasn't like the other orgasm. All golden, nice and pretty. This was dark and wicked and powerful, and she was going to use dirty words and swear and promise many things that she had never promised to a man before, and…

Oh, yes…

His chest was heaving. Great, large exertions. A builder's chest, a builder's cock.

He was pulling her apart, splitting her in two. Every time she thought she was there, he'd thrust even harder, pushing her further than any human being could possibly survive. The orgasm was there, building between her legs, in her throat. With one mighty thrust, he tore deep inside her, beyond the womb, beyond the mind, beyond the heart. Jenna shoved a fist in her mouth and swallowed a scream. Finally, *finally*, she came.

CAM WAS HEAVY and large and slightly sweaty, and partially comatose. Jenna had never felt anything so beautiful. She could smell the soapy shampoo that he used, the tangy underpinnings of male sweat and the musky smell of sex.

"That was awesome," said Jenna, and then giggled. Oh, man, she was regressing.

"More than that."

"Cam?"

"Don't ask me to move. I can't."

"I don't feel my legs."

He pinched her on the ass. "Can you feel that?"

"Are you on medication?"

"Nope." He lifted his face, and flashed her the world's goofiest grin. "Just one horny man and one very naughty doc."

Weakly, Jenna lifted a hand and slapped him on the back. There was no hostility, more of I-need-to-touch-your-body tickle. "Cam?"

He took her mouth and started to kiss her. Her muscles began to stir, his cock began to stir. Just when she was sure she couldn't fully appreciate this, that her muscles were too atrophied to move, he slipped inside her and she began to fully appreciate it. Jenna's juices began to stir again.

The human body was a miraculous thing.

Who knew?

April 1, 3:00 a.m.

THREE HOURS LATER, they'd moved from the couch to the floor. Jenna had lost the shoes and the hose, Cam had lost his mind several times over. Part of him knew why she was here, knew that he shouldn't be all so tongue-wagging happy about it, that he should be plotting his escape to the boat race. But a naked woman should never be ignored. When she was intelligent, ambitious and smoking hot, as well, it made ignoring her impossible.

His randy cock agreed.

Still, in spite of the sex, his watch had stayed on, and eventually he was going to have to move. Midnight was fast approaching; he was going to have to leave.

"Why don't you lose the watch?"

The way she said it, it was all so innocent, all so completely without motive, but the doc did nothing without motive, without altruistic purpose.

Cam, on the other hand, had no such scruples.

He rolled her underneath him, his mouth latching onto her breast. She loved that, her head falling back, her mouth falling slack, her dark lashes falling low, and Cam was not one to deny a woman her pleasure. First one breast, then another, until she rolled on top of him, forcibly removing his mouth, gasping for breath.

"My turn," she said, taking both his hands, and pulling them over his head.

He raised his brows. "Kinky."

"You haven't seen kinky," she promised, but he felt the tug at his watchband, and he knew where this particular game was headed.

Cam pulled his hands free and grabbed her up, heading for the bedroom.

"Not quite yet."

April 1, 3:10 a.m.

OUTSIDE, the moon was high in the sky, it was well into April first, and so far there were no disasters. Not unless you counted the collapse of her nervous system. Jenna was now comfortably tucked into the perfectly healthy shoulder of Cam and she wanted to keep it that way. For another nine hours.

All she needed was a few moments alone. "Do you have some ice?"

"Ice?"

"Yes. Ice. It's very hot in here. I'm thinking ice water would be nice."

"And you want me to get it for you?" he asked.

"That's the way things work in polite America."

"Why should I trust you?"

"With ice?"

He sighed and lifted his arm, and she kept the triumph from her smile.

"Okay, be right back." She watched his easy movements with greedy eyes as he slid out of bed. Quite simply, he was magnificent. Long, tight muscles that rippled when he moved. He had a workman's tan on his arms and around his neck.

She pretended (it wasn't hard) to ogle him and luxuriate in the sated afterglow of sex (again, not hard) until he left the room. Then she climbed out of bed, unplugging the clock next to the bed, angling it to face the wall.

One down. Now to get the watch.

He seemed excessively attached to that watch, or more likely, he didn't trust her. Cam was very perceptive that way. But he had underestimated the power of her determination to keep him alive…and sexually active.

She remembered the gleaming gold metal on the band and smiled, sauntering into the bathroom and turning on the shower. "Cam?"

He appeared in the doorway, naked, carrying a glass of frosty ice water. "You want a shower?"

"I think so," she said and walked into the glass enclosure, letting the warm water blast over her.

"I thought you were hot."

She reached for the soap and shrugged, watching his eyes skim down her body. "I feel…dirty."

He swallowed, his face perhaps a little pale. She grabbed the soap and had a fine time getting clean, paying particular attention to her chest.

Diligently she washed, creating great mounds of frothy white bubbles that dripped from her breasts. Her hands stroked and rubbed and tweaked, doing a fine job of ignoring his labored breathing. Then she found the particularly dirty place between her legs and she proceeded to rub.

These were not normal Jenna Ferrar moves. She had an image, a reputation to uphold, but here, with Cam, that all faded away like yesterday's memories. Tonight, she'd let down her hair, and discovered a part of her personality she didn't realize she had.

It was the burning look in his eyes that spurred her on, and Jenna knew she should be focused on getting Cam in the shower with her, getting him to take off the watch, but she was feeling remarkably at ease in this carnal playground.

It had been so long. It had been never.

Her finger slid inside her, stroking her clit, teasing him, and it felt so gloriously freeing. Cam didn't move, his erection heavy, thick, pulsing for her, and she felt the swelling in her body that understood.

Desire.

Her lips curved with it, her nipples peaked with it, and her mind was drunk with it.

"Come play with me," she taunted.

He shook his head. "You're doing fine." He moved his hand over his cock, and Jenna gulped.

"Suit yourself," she said, and adjusting the water velocity, adjusting the angle, letting the hard jets pulsate over her breasts, she began to play in earnest.

Jenna knew her body, knew the way she needed to be touched, knew the exact length of time to get her to orgasm, but this wasn't functional stress relief. This was pleasing him, seducing him.

Pleasing her.

The hard lash of the warm water stoked her arousal and she moaned.

With his free hand, Cam reached out, obviously wanting to touch her, and she smiled, her invitation blatant because her puny finger was no substitute for thick, heavy male.

The air was misty, a cloak of almost-privacy kept him away from her, and Jenna stroked harder, feeling the first twinge of orgasm.

It wasn't enough.

Right now, she didn't want to be alone. "Please," she

told him, and watched as he stripped off his watch, stepped into the shower and backed her to the wall. She nearly climbed him in her hurry, and then, she felt it. Felt him.

Thick, heavy, pushing, filling.

His hands wrapped under her ass, and there was nowhere to hold, and he moved hard and fast. She loved the wild look of him, the tense muscles in his jaw, the way his eyes locked on to hers. Jenna could feel the orgasm building inside her, begging for release. And when the dam inside her broke, she called out his name. She had no idea that she could feel this much pleasure, this much trust. Her muscles spasmed around him, and his body froze, his arms like bands around her. For a moment she stayed, impaled and boneless, shudders of satisfaction playing like an echo, again and again.

Cam lifted his head. Tensed.

"What's wrong?" she asked.

Gently he let her go and handed her a towel. His eyes had lost that openness from before. Now he looked trapped and haunted. And the buzzing wouldn't stop.

"What's that?"

Cam's smile held no trace of humor. His eyes met hers before he looked away.

"It's the fire alarm. The Curse. I have to get out of here."

5

April 1, 4:00 a.m.

AFTER HE THREW ON A pair of jeans, Cam dug around his bedroom, searching for the duffel bag he'd packed earlier, but was now nowhere to be found. Frantic, he dumped the sheets on the floor, and Jenna's scent was in those sheets, flooding his senses. The buzzing from the building's fire alarm cleaved through his head like an axe.

Goddamn, he needed to leave. It was April Fools' and he could feel the tension coiling inside him. This fear was the main reason he took April Fools' on his own terms, in his own way.

He'd call the car service, and what the hell did they care if it was 4:00 a.m. or 9:00 a.m.? But first he needed to find the damn bag.

It wasn't under the bed, under his clothes or tossed casually in his closet. It wasn't anywhere.

While he tore his apartment apart, his skin starting to crawl. He couldn't look at Jenna. He didn't want to see her, wrapped only in his towel, watching him with her curiously detached doctor's eyes.

Watching Cam fall apart.

He'd known this was a mistake. His heart was pounding double time in his chest, sweat was pooling on his neck. Why didn't somebody shut off the alarm?

Her fingers touched the bare skin of his back, and Cam whipped around to face her. He could feel the adrenaline pumping through him, destroying him.

"What?" he asked, hearing the jagged edge to his words. Hating it.

"I didn't mean to startle you," she said, crisp and cool in a voice meant to soothe.

"My bag was here. I swear. Did you take it?" It was a wholly paranoid question, the fevered imagination of a not-quite-lucid mind. In high-stress situations, people expected jagged nerves and heightened reflexes. In his own apartment, it only made him look weak.

Jenna continued to study him with those non-judgmental eyes, and in many ways, it was a helluva lot worse.

"I didn't take it. The watch was pretty much the extent of my derring-do. Oh, and I unplugged the clock."

It was the first time he noticed the way the normally positioned clock was turned toward the wall. He'd been so caught up in her that he hadn't noticed. Not that it mattered, and finally—finally—the alarm ground to a halt.

His heart resumed a less frantic pace, but still, the memory of the cackling bleat of the noise remained in his head, and he grabbed a handful of aspirin from a bottle on his nightstand, tilted back his head, swallowing the pills quickly.

"You're always like this?" she quietly asked.

"No. Only if I wait it out. I don't like to wait. That's

why I usually get a jump on it, doing something crazy before the curse gets a jump on me."

"Cam…" she started, and then stopped. He understood. There wasn't anything to say.

His vision began to blur, the world starting to circle around him, sucking him in. He stumbled backward, tripping over the bed, and that was all he knew.

IT WAS AN HOUR LATER before Jenna's blood pressure returned to something close to normal. Now she sat stiffly in his bed, Cam curled in her lap, his eyes blessedly closed. He was asleep.

The idiot was lucky that it was cold medicine he'd grabbed, not something more lethal. Still, at least it brought him the peace he so desperately needed.

Finally she understood.

Her hand stroked through his hair, studying the dark lashes that lay so innocently on his cheek. Like a boy.

The stubble on his jaw proclaimed something more. As did the marks on her breasts.

The buzzer on his apartment rang forty-seven times, his cell beeped incessantly until she turned it off. There was a broken water pipe on the floor above, and the spreading stain on the ceiling was almost hypnotic to watch grow, but Jenna didn't leave.

She stayed in Cam's bed, holding him in her arms, stroking his hair and jealously guarding his sleep.

She'd come here expecting to help him, to save him from his devils, but instead, she'd found something new. A piece of herself that she liked, that she enjoyed, that she treasured.

Mentally, she high-fived the loose harlot that she'd discovered inside. Right now, she felt relaxed, alive, desired.

She owed him more than he ever knew. When he woke up, she'd tell him that. For now, she leaned down and pressed a warm kiss to his mouth.

Exhausted from lack of sleep, Jenna closed her eyes, hearing the buzzer ring. Let whoever it was believe that Cam Franklin wasn't home. Let them think that Cam Franklin was somewhere out risking life and limb.

Right now, there was only one task for her, and it was a big one. While on her watch, Cam was finally going to be safe.

6

CAM WOKE SLOWLY, scanning the disaster site that had been his bedroom, but there were no injuries, no blood. He pushed his face into his pillow and smiled.

No pillow.

Jenna.

He pressed a grateful kiss to the inviting skin, and then frowned as the previous night's events clicked back into place.

The clock was now on, and he realized it was 12:27 a.m. on April 2. Cautiously he flexed his hands—no bruising, no fractures. The rest of him seemed to be fine, too.

Had he slept through the entire day? Nah. It was impossible.

"Hey, Sleeping Beauty," she murmured, turning on the light.

Jenna.

He lifted his head, unhappy to notice that she was sleeping in his bed with her red dress back on. Not that it had to stay on.

"Did it go away?"

She knew what he was talking about. The Curse. It

with a capital *I.* "You slept the entire day. Welcome to April Two."

"You're sure."

She clicked on the television, and he watched the date and time crawl on the news channel. She was right.

"I have some connections, but not that good."

"What happened?"

"You grabbed the cold medicine instead of aspirin."

Groggily he rubbed his head. "I don't have cold medicine."

"Apparently you've forgotten about it, because it's here," she replied.

The words played in his head, new implications, new ideas, new plans. Plans with Jenna. Cam sat up, stretched his arms, feeling amazingly good. "I can't believe it—April second."

"Live and in person."

"And nothing bad happened?"

"You might need a need roof at some point," she stated, pointing to the wet patch on the ceiling.

"No HazMat scares, no mislaid laundry, no misdelivered packages of live snakes?"

"Sure, there were a few things."

"Bad?"

"You should have seen me with the IRS auditor. Masterful. He won't be back." She smiled at him then, not so cool, not so detached, and a charge of lust shot through to his groin.

"You really stayed all day? Why?"

Her hands plucked at the sheets of his bed, a faint blush on her cheeks. "For the great sex."

"Like there was any doubt," he said, because sex was the least of his problems.

She gently laid a hand over his. "And for you. You don't have to do this alone."

Casually Cam rolled his shoulders, a nonchalant gesture to indicate that it had never mattered whether he was alone or not. Jenna stared at him as if she didn't believe him. Cam didn't mind.

"I'm kinda liking having my own personal doc. It's convenient."

"And cheap."

"Are we talking frugal or tawdry?"

This time, she rolled a shoulder, a nonchalant gesture to indicate that it didn't matter, and he covered her mouth, not so nonchalant, because it mattered.

She mattered.

He pulled her close, held her tight, fiercely tight, feeling the quiver within her. That quiet shudder always gave her away.

"Doc?"

Jenna looked at him, and despite the dim of the room, he saw something warm and good. Something that made him realize he would never be the same. "Yeah?" she asked.

Cam hesitated for a minute then shook off his nerves. "You don't think less of me?"

"Why should I?"

"Because of the panic attacks," he answered, not that he didn't think she needed the answer. She was a doc. She knew. He loved that she understood him and accepted him, but Cam wasn't sure he accepted himself. "Nobody knows. My family doesn't even know."

"You should tell them."

"I like my other image better."

She quirked a brow at him, haughty and all-knowing. In fact, if it wasn't for the sexy little love bite right below her neck, he might have been more offended. "The other image? You mean the stupid guy that takes death-defying risks?"

"That's not exactly the image I was thinking about." He liked being the solid rock of the family. Would John Wayne suffer anxiety attacks? Probably not.

"Why don't you be you? Do what you want to do, not what you think you have to do."

Her dark eyes were loving when she looked at him, as if she didn't care who he was. Actually, at the moment, lying next to her, feeling her fingers locked around his, he didn't mind being who he was. It was nice to be taken care of for once.

"What if I want to dive out of an airplane on April first?"

Jenna put on her bossy doctor's face, exactly like he'd hoped she would. He liked that face. He'd liked it from the first time he'd met her. "Do the skydiving on April second," she instructed. "Play golf on April first. Or, alternatively, if you want to lounge in bed on April first, then maybe you should do that."

His fingers slid along her neck, underneath her dress, and whoops, accidentally exposed one shoulder. She had great shoulders. Soft, capable, sexy. "Lounging in bed is a very tempting idea. You'd be there?"

"Would you like me to be there?" she asked, and he noticed the uncertainty in her eyes. Amazing that with all the letters after her name, after all the lives she'd saved, she still hadn't clued in to how he felt.

He took her face in his hands, kissing her gently and sincere. "Yes."

"Then, I'd be there."

Well satisfied with life at the moment, Cam leaned back against the pillows and pulled her into his arms, accidentally exposing the other shoulder, as well. "I'll miss the E.R. I sort of liked the fights with Bertie. And I loved when you put your hands on me. Those were some good memories."

"We can make new memories. Better memories," she told him, and oops, there went the dress, and they spent the next few hours making new memories. Definitely better memories.

It was a long time later before Cam found the exact right instant, when the morning sun was warm on the bed sheets, when the city was humming outside, sounding so very far away, and when Jenna was curled against him, her hand resting over his heart.

"Thank you," he whispered.

"For what?"

Cam stayed silent for a minute because he wasn't good at this. Wasn't good at talking about things that were inside him. Fears. Emotions. But he felt too good, too much at peace.

"I always handled the First so badly, my heart always got so fried, pumping like mad, and there wasn't any room for anyone or anything. But I don't want to do anything next year. I just want to be here. With you. I thought my heart had to stay the other way forever. But it's different today. It feels good, strong, not so anxious. You fixed that."

She raised her head, resting her chin on his chest. "You're the one who fixed it."

No, he thought, and he noticed that her hand still rested on his heart, soothing it, calming it, fixing it. She had done that, but he knew better that to argue with the doc. So he kissed her instead, showing her how much he cared. Someday she'd figure it out. She was smart that way. She was the doc. His doc.

She'd figure that one out, too, someday, because she was smart that way. Very, very smart.

* * * * *

DARCY'S DARK DAY
Julie Kenner

1

April Fools' Day, three years ago

Train arrives Union Station 8:15.
Will bring bagels.

DARCY'S FINGERS HOVERED over the send button, knowing she was being an absolute chickenshit. If she had any sort of backbone whatsoever, she'd dial the phone instead and tell her big brother Cam that she was in town, and she was going to walk boldly through subway stations—even getting close to the edge. She was going to jaywalk in front of speeding taxis, and walk by herself through Central Park. She was going to eat from street vendors without carrying antacids, and she was going to go all the way up to the top of the Empire State Building and look waaaaay down to the ground below.

She was going to do all of that, and she was going to be *fine,* dammit, because the whole idea of a family curse was just silly. Life had order and reason and mathematical certainties. Nature was about symmetry and patterns, *not* about random happenstance and curses, and none of her doom-and-gloom siblings were going to change that.

So why aren't you dialing the phone? Why are you sending a text?

She scowled at the little voice in her head—a voice that sounded remarkably like herself. And she answered herself firmly. *Because it's early. He's probably still asleep.*

It's tricky lying to oneself, the problem being that she knew, even as she was saying it, that it was a lie. Cam was Mr. Early-Riser. Mr. Meet-and-Greet-the-Day. Especially *this* day, one he met in grave defiance annually. And, she had to reluctantly admit, one he usually met with injury.

It was a self-fulfilling prophecy, she told herself firmly, reaching down to hook her purse strap over her arm as the garbled voice over the loudspeaker announced the imminent arrival of the train at the station. Cam's history of nasty April first E.R. visits was the direct result of her brother being a complete and total idiot about that particular day. If you go out and put yourself in harm's way, harm would find you. Cam's spate of bad luck wasn't the product of a curse so much as the product of poor planning and carelessness. Considering how he always went out of his way to defy fate, it was a statistical certainty that his defiance would terminate with injury. He never saw it that way, though. She'd argued, diagrammed and even scrawled long, complex mathematical formulas, knowing her older brother couldn't make heads nor tails of the symbols, but still hoping to impress him with the seriousness of her conclusions. *Trust me, I'm a mathematician.*

Hadn't ever worked. Not with Cam or Reg or Devon.

It was, she thought, the reason she'd decided to study

mathematics in the first place—because of the purity of numbers. They didn't change because it was October 12 or March 16 or April 1. Numbers knew their place; numbers knew the rules. And numbers were the key to the universe—everything in the world could be reduced to simple mathematics. Even humans were the product of a near-infinite division of cells.

Superstitions and curses had no place in such an orderly universe, and because Darcy knew that—even if her siblings didn't—she'd decided to study what she already knew was true.

Reason and order, those were her mottoes.

But no matter how hard she tried to explain to her siblings that the curse was nothing more than a statistical anomaly skewed because of familial expectations, her brothers and sister still only saw a curse. At first, Darcy thought they blew her off because she was the youngest, in the way that big sisters and brothers do. But she was twenty-six now, and had been living on her own in Massachusetts attending MIT for the last seven years, through undergrad and now into her doctorate program. Even her siblings could no longer look at her as a kid.

Well, that wasn't true. She was still a kid to them, and always would be. But they trusted her intellect. They trusted what she knew about numbers and reason.

But they didn't trust her about the curse, even though she knew she was right. She *had* to be right, because if a curse could exist in a world organized by numbers and reason, then that meant that there was no order or reason. And where did that leave her? Where did that leave every other scientist and mathematician, for that matter?

She tried to explain all of that to her siblings, to absolutely no avail. They saw only what they wanted, and because of that, they fell victim, blaming every bad thing that happened to them on April first on some mythical curse thrust upon the family in days gone by.

Honestly.

A lanky guy in desperate need of deodorant flopped into the seat beside her, then grinned, his teeth a bilious yellow. She forced herself not to crinkle her nose, then focused hard on her phone. It still showed two bars of signal, and she pressed Send before she could talk herself out of it. Less than a minute later, the phone started to ring. She waited, and the signal bars faded. Voice mail had picked up.

She told herself it wasn't that she didn't want to talk to her brother—it was just that she didn't want to talk to him about the Franklin Curse. Or, at least, she didn't want to talk to him about it without the fortification of bagels and coffee.

For that matter, maybe she should rethink the whole bagel thing. If she went by his apartment, would he let her out again?

The truth was, she'd come into New York City today in one more attempt to prove her point: that April Fools' Day was perfectly safe. And so she had to see him. Because otherwise, why come, other than to see her best friend and go shopping and then to a show? But those were all the incidental perks. The real point of being here today was to walk through the city, physically proving her ultimate theorem that there was no curse.

She'd already proved that to herself, though.

Which meant she had to call Cam. He had to stand witness to her lack of bad fortune.

Now that she was here, though, she had to admit that maybe this hadn't been the best plan. After all, Cam truly believed, and he truly loved her. Which meant he'd go to any lengths to see her safe.

She had a sudden vision of the inside of a broom closet, and frowned. Surely, he wouldn't really…

In the past, she wouldn't have worried. It was just Cam back then. But now he had Jenna, and as much as Darcy loved her new sister-in-law, she also knew that Jenna was now a believer, and would undoubtedly assist Cam in locking Darcy in a padded room until after midnight. Just to keep her safe.

"You're not careful enough," Cam had told her only two weeks ago. Darcy had snorted loudly. He was one to talk, Mr. I-Think-I'll-Build-a-Rocket-to-Mars-and-Defy-Fate.

But she had to admit that he'd always believed in the curse—he'd just always faced it down.

Not Darcy. She knew bullshit when she saw it. If there was really some horrible curse affecting all four of the Franklin kids, then shouldn't one of her elder siblings be dead by now? A morbid thought, maybe, but true. A theorem required proof, not coincidences masquerading as proof.

No, the only reason her siblings were constantly getting April Fool injuries lay with the name of the day: they were fools. Fools who believed they'd have bad luck, and so, poof, they did.

The *clackety-clack* of the train took on a slower rhythm, and she rose, realizing as she did that her purse felt significantly lighter. She glanced at it, then realized there was no *it* to see. All she had was a strap, now hanging loosely over her shoulder, the ends neatly sliced, as if by a razor. The purse itself was gone, and so was the stinky guy with yellow teeth.

A small niggle of something familiar started to whisper in the back of her head. A voice that once again sounded like her.

A voice that was saying, *"I told you so."*

Well, hell.

THE RINGING PHONE TAUNTED Evan from across the room. Usually, he left it by his bedside, and he could easily roll over and answer it. Last night—at the tail end of his fit of productivity—he'd left the thing sitting on his desk, which happened to be located exactly eleven feet from his bed. He knew, because he'd meticulously measured the seven hundred and fifteen square-foot condo six years ago before he'd decided to open a vein and bleed money into the Manhattan real-estate market.

The phone rang again. Eleven feet, zero inches. Not an overwhelming distance, but one that would require him to get out of bed.

He really didn't want to get out of bed.

Another ring.

Shit.

With a groan, he rolled to face the offending instrument, wishing Ma Bell—or whoever was in charge these days—came with valet service. A Jeeves to walk the phone to him on a silver platter and announce that Mr. So-and-So was calling. Or, better, to tell him that a telemarketer was on the line, and that Evan shouldn't trouble himself and to please, sir, go back to sleep.

Riiiiinnnnng.

He closed his eyes and waited while the closest thing

he had to his fantasy Jeeves picked up the line. *"Hi, you've reached Evan Olsen with Midtown Magazine. I'm unavailable right now, but please leave a message and I'll call you back as soon as I can."*

"Yo, Evan. You there? It's Cam. Pick up. I've got a crisis."

His buddy's voice filled the room, and Evan crossed those eleven feet without even thinking about it. "Hey. I'm here. Shit, it's April first. You battered and broken?"

Cam cleared his throat, and Evan knew that his friend had in fact suffered his annual injury. That wasn't necessarily a bad thing—it was those injuries that had brought Cam and Jenna together—but Evan couldn't help but shake his head. The Franklin Family Curse. Evan was a believer, and he wasn't even a member of the family, just a longtime friend.

No, it was more than that. He was a friend, yes, but he was also wrapped up in the curse. Cam had joked that Evan got the yin while the Franklins got the yang, but Evan knew better. He'd gotten the short end of the stick, too. He just couldn't tell anyone.

What had happened was that he'd stood up for Cam one April first against the wrath of Cam's mother, and somehow Evan had walked away a hero, with all the perks that came with it—those particular perks for a fifteen-year-old being much attention from girls. Good on the surface, maybe, but not underneath.

Before that, he'd been just another guy. Noticed, because he played football and was Cam Franklin's friend, but nothing special. After, though, he was The Man.

He'd be lying if he didn't admit he'd enjoyed the

role, but after a while, he wanted to simply be himself. But the mythology was there, and there'd been nowhere to hide.

That's what happens when you play hero in a small town. When you follow your best friend to the river during a storm on April Fools' day.

When your cursed best friend decides to swim the width of the river, despite everyone in town knowing how dangerous that river was when the water rose.

And when you haul him back to shore, and then lie to his mother and say that Cam wasn't trying to defy the curse by swimming across the damn river. That he'd fallen off the bridge—the curse, sure, but not him defying it—and you'd jumped in to rescue him.

Selfless, they'd all said.

Heroic, they'd all cheered.

But he knew the truth. He should never have let Cam try to swim across in the first place. Should never have let his best friend put himself in the position of needing to be rescued.

Evan hadn't been a hero, he'd been a damned accomplice. But he couldn't tell anyone that without getting Cam in hip-deep trouble with his parents.

So he'd taken his licks, and let the town fete him. And what should have been a great thing ended up being a miserable burden.

In fact, that's part of the reason why he'd become a reporter. Not simply to look at the surface of things, but to dig until he could see how different it really was down below. Because who better than him to know that there was always another story going on beneath the surface?

He pulled himself out of his reverie and concentrated

on his friend. "So what did you do?" he asked. "SCUBA dive without a regulator? Sky dive without a parachute?"

"I'm reformed, haven't you heard? All I did was trip over the damn cat. Twisted my ankle and threw my back out just after midnight. I've been on the couch all night."

"You need me to come over?"

"Yeah," Cam said. "But not for me. For Darcy."

Evan's knees suddenly weren't quite strong enough to support him, and he sank down on the edge of the bed, the phone still clutched to his ear. "Darcy? She's okay, right?"

Darcy was Cam's little sister, the youngest of the four Franklin kids. And although Evan had been Cameron Franklin's best friend throughout high school and college, it had always been Darcy who'd got his pulse rate going. Darcy who had been his fantasy. Darcy, whom he could never approach. Because how could he go after his best friend's little sister?

"Right now she's fine," Cam was saying. "But the day is young, and it's not a great day to be a Franklin in New York."

"She's here?" He hadn't seen her in years. He could still remember the first time he'd met her—he'd been a senior and she'd been by herself, alone at a table in the cafeteria. He'd come in with Cam, the two of them surrounded as usual by laughing friends—cheerleaders and jocks and a few kids from band. Cam had noticed her across the room and called her name. She'd slowly put her finger in the book to mark her page, then looked up, her eyes wide and unblinking and so bright they seemed to cut right through Evan. "Wanna sit with us?" Cam had asked. She'd smiled, then shook her head and returned casually to her book. The shock of the rejection had reverberated through the cafeteria. No one—*no one*—turned down an offer to dine with Cam and his friends.

No one except Darcy.

She'd gained a bit of respect from the rest of the school that day, and also a bit of a reputation as a freak. The fact that she was young for a freshman—having skipped a year of junior high—didn't help, and for the most part, Darcy Franklin had become a school loner, even with one of the most popular guys in school as a brother.

Evan, however, had been smitten the first time he'd seen her. He'd never done anything about it, though. He might have had his own entourage of hero-worshipping girls, but the idea of going after Cam's little sister—and a freshman, no less—was unthinkable. So he'd consoled himself with talking to her after school at Cam's house, arguing about cool books they'd read, like the works of Stephen Hawkings or Carl Sagan. After he graduated, he'd see her occasionally on the local college campus, taking dual-credit courses. Each time, he'd feel that familiar twist in his gut, but again, he never did anything about it. She was a high-school girl, and he was in college. She was still Cam's sister. And he was dating an English major he'd met at registration.

Now, the English major and Evan had gone their separate ways, Darcy was all grown up and the simple sound of her name still made his skin tingle. "She's in the city?" he asked. The last he'd heard, she was at MIT working toward a Ph.D. in mathematics.

"On the way to my apartment," Cam said. "And unless my little sister has changed, there's no way I'm going to convince her to stay here for the day."

"What do you want me to do?" Already he was out of bed. Already, he was imagining a day with Darcy.

"I need you watch out for her, buddy," Cam said, voicing the words that Evan so wanted to here. "I need you to take care of her. I know it's a lot to ask—following my kid sister around—but I'd really appreciate it if—"

"No worries," Evan said, his voice in a rush. "I get it. You're worried about her. She's alone in the city on April first."

"The kid's brilliant," Cam said. "But she can be scattered. And tunnel-visioned. And she's determined to pretend like the curse doesn't exist."

"Don't worry," Evan said. "I'll keep an eye on her."

"How?"

"Huh?"

"She'll have both our butts in a sling if she realizes I asked you to keep an eye on her. And it's not like you're going to play James Bond in a trenchcoat and tail her from afar. So what's your excuse going to be? To hang out with her, I mean."

"Right," Evan said, scrambling. "I'll think of something." Heck yes, he'd think of something. The idea of spending the day with Darcy beat pretty much anything else he could think of doing that day, and that included winning the lottery.

"How about an article?" Cam said. "Tell her you're doing a feature on the family curse."

"That'll go over well," Evan said. He might believe in the curse—how could he not?—but he knew damn good and well that Darcy was the hold-out in the family. And the truth was that antagonizing her wasn't what he had in mind. No, his image of the perfect day was something significantly different.

"She says she doesn't believe in the curse," Cam said. "But she can't deny what happens to us every year."

"I'll tell her I want to write a feature piece from her perspective. Holding the line in a family of believers."

"You're a good man," Cam said. "There's no one I trust more to keep an eye on my baby sister."

An eye, Evan thought. He'd keep an eye on her, all right. On those flashing green eyes and that mass of wild, untamable curls.

He imagined brushing her hair out of her eyes and stroking her cheek, taking her hand and walking through the park. Sharing a kiss on the top of the Empire State Building.

And, yeah, he imagined a hell of a lot more than that, too.

Cam sighed. "It's just that she can be so damn naive, you know? I don't want her to get hurt."

"Right," Evan said, reining in all of his fantasies, because he could have none of them. This was *Darcy* he was thinking about. Cam's little sister, who'd never once shown the slightest hint of interest in him. "I'll keep her safe."

Safe, he thought. And at arm's length.

2

"YOUR PURSE WAS STOLEN," Cam said. He spoke the words as if they constituted mathematical proof, and punctuated them with a scowl, the effect of which was only slightly lessened by the flower-print blanket Jenna had tucked around his shoulders, his body and his elevated foot.

"So? Lots of people get robbed in New York without being cursed. All it means is that I was an idiot for not holding the thing closer. And," she added with a wry grin, "it means I need to borrow some cash."

"And if I say no?" Cam asked, as if that was his trump card.

She rolled her eyes. "I only need to borrow a few bucks. As soon as the bank opens, I can get more." She reached into the back pocket of her jeans and pulled out her driver's license. "I always keep it in my pocket when I'm in the city. I figure that's just smart."

"You're being irresponsible," Cam said, apparently unimpressed by her foresight. "Stay here, nice and tight and snug. Tomorrow you can window shop or do whatever you planned on doing."

"Tomorrow, I'm going back home. And I don't want to stay in today. I have theater tickets for tonight, and

I'm going. They're for *Dance in the Winter*, and it's sold out for the next two years. It's the hottest thing on Broadway right now, and I'm not missing it. Just because you're laid up on the couch doesn't mean I have to be an invalid, too."

"It's hours until your show," Jenna said, coming back into the room with a yellow tray topped with three mugs of coffee. "And Cam and I hardly ever see you."

"Jenna's right," Cam said, taking one of the mugs, then wincing when hot coffee sloshed over the sides onto his hand. Darcy eyed the tray and decided to wait. "Hang out here and keep us company," Cam added.

"Keep you company?" she repeated. "Cameron Franklin? Mr. Action? Laid up in bed with a sprained ankle, and you want me to just hang out here for the day? Excuse me for being blunt, but that's really not my idea of a good time."

"I sprained it this morning, Darcy. Right after midnight." He ran his fingers through his thick hair, making it stand up in tufts and giving him the look of a man who knew he was fighting a losing battle, but was determined to go on fighting. "You know what day this is. Why the hell did you have to come in to New York today, anyway?"

"Because tonight's the play," she said simply. And that was true, since she'd specifically told her friend Bella to buy tickets for the April 1 show. "And because I was able to take the whole day for shopping. It's not like my schedule gives me that many free days. MIT's not exactly a party school, you know."

Also true, but what she didn't point out was that as a Ph.D. candidate, she had significantly more flexibility than she'd had during the earlier years of her education. Her free time was still sadly lacking, but at least she could move the blocks of time around, like tiles on a sliding-number puzzle, until she managed to create a gap large enough to allow for a trip into the city.

But was it really her brother's business if she got a certain sense of satisfaction from coming to New York City on this day?

Cam used to dive out of planes on April Fools' Day—his boldness a way of thumbing his nose at the curse. Darcy did the same. Only she wasn't daring the curse—there was no curse, after all. Instead, she was proving a point to her siblings who continued to believe in such nonsense.

"Dammit, Darcy," Cam said, not needing to say any more. She understood his frustration. She even sympathized with it. However silly it might be, Cam was a believer, and her big brother's concern was genuine.

"Bella's going to be with me all day," she said, bringing up her undergraduate roommate the way a Civil War officer might have raised a white flag. "We're going to shop, have lunch, shop more, then do drinks and the theater. So I won't be out in the big, bad city on my own." She shrugged. "That's the best deal I can offer."

"It's not—"

Jenna put a hand on his shoulder, effectively silencing her husband. "Promise us you'll be careful?"

"I already have," Darcy said. "But if it'll make you feel better, I'll promise again. If you have any of those old family documents that Reg is always digging up, I'll even swear on those. I'll do whatever you want to make you believe I'll be safe—except spend the day locked up in here with you," she added, as Cam started to open his mouth.

"At least stay for breakfast," Jenna said. "You brought the bagels. I can scramble some eggs, fry up some sausage."

Darcy shook her head. "No, thanks. I want to get going. I just—" She cut herself off. She couldn't exactly admit that she'd done this on purpose, coming here today, knowing that he'd spend the long hours worried about her. She'd come, because it would have that much more impact when she survived the day unscathed. Afterward, it's just a story. Knowing before had meant her brother would be involved, too. And maybe this would finally convince him.

Maybe, she thought. But as she glanced ruefully at his raised ankle, she had to admit she doubted that he'd ever become a non-believer.

It took another twenty minutes for Darcy to extricate herself from her brother and sister-in-law, and that included fifteen for more arguing and five to search for her driver's license, even though she could have sworn she'd put it back in her pocket. She finally found it in the cushions of a nearby armchair that she didn't even remember sitting in. She took two long gulps of the now cold coffee, dribbled enough on her white shirt that she had to beg a replacement from Jenna and finally managed to get out the door and breathe a sigh of relief that at nine forty-five, her day was about to begin.

And, dammit, it was a day that promised to be curse-free, carefree and fun.

The elevator did not stick as she descended to the lobby from Cameron's apartment. She didn't slip on the newly waxed floor, and no armed thug rushed the building, prepared to take everyone in the lobby hostage. In fact, the first few moments away from her big brother were so uniquely dull and uneventful that she half considered calling him from the house phone and telling him that a flock of angry penguins had stormed the building, knocked her over and now her picture was going to be splashed all over the front page of the *Post* with a decadent headline about how an MIT Ph.D. candidate was caught in a torrid penguin lovefest in the lobby of one of Manhattan's most exclusive apartment buildings.

Or maybe not.

She shifted, intending to swing her purse over her arm, then realized she didn't have a purse. She patted her back pocket, feeling her driver's license and the fifty-dollar bill that Cam had handed her. She didn't even realize she'd been glancing down as she stepped past the doorman until she glanced back up and felt the sharp stab to her heart. Not the bad you've-been-mugged-on-the-streets-of-Manhattan kind of stab, but the good man-of-your-fantasies-staring-right-at-you kind of stab. The kind that's hot and cold at the same time and makes your skin go all prickly and your knees go week and your mouth go dry.

The kind of stab that Darcy got whenever she looked at Evan Olsen—and this time, he was looking right back.

He stood for a moment—and for one exquisite instant it seemed that he was as desperate for her as she was for him—then a wide grin broke out across his face, and the desire she'd imagined shifted into the familiar, friendly expression she'd seen so many times on her big brother's best friend's face. "Darcy! Hey! I'm so glad I caught you."

Hope fluttered through her, and she took a step toward him, intending to speak, but no words coming out because her mouth was suddenly full of cotton. Or sandpaper. Or sandpaper wrapped in cotton.

"Darcy?"

She coughed. "Sorry. Thinking. I've been working on this algorithm, and—"

"And suddenly the blank expression makes tons of sense."

She laughed. "I swear it's a really fascinating algorithm."

"Aren't they all?" he asked, completely deadpan.

"Are you here to see Cam?" she asked, which was a totally inane thing to say since—duh—he was standing right outside Cam's apartment and they'd been best friends for years. He sure as hell wasn't there to see her.

"Actually, I was on my way to see you."

And there it was—the last prime number, all the digits of pi, the nirvana to end all nirvanas.

This was the man she'd had fantasies about since her first day of high school. The guy who'd been at the center of so much female attention during school. She smiled to herself, remembering how the girls had flocked around him, the hero of the town.

They'd all been jealous of her, being the sister to Evan's best friend. At first, she'd never had the guts to talk to him when she saw him at the house. Then they'd started talking, about math or politics or whatever. Stupid stuff. Nothing personal, nothing intimate.

But in her imagination...

Oh, my.

She'd imagined his face during long, slow soaks in

the tub. She'd replayed their conversations, twisting their arguments around and analyzing his point of view. She rarely shifted off her own opinion, but she liked the way he thought.

And then she'd let the imaginary conversation drift away in favor of the magical illusion of his hands on her as she lay naked between cool, crisp sheets.

He'd filled her mind for years, even though he'd never once filled her bed.

Wow.

The guy. This was that guy—and he was right there, smiling at her.

Forget the curse—April Fools' Day should be gold-plated and set up on the mantle.

She realized she was gaping, played the conversation back in her head, and said the first—albeit idiotic—thing that came to mind. "You're here to see *me?* Um, why?"

He laughed. "Can't I just want to see you?"

"No." The word came out fast, and she backtracked. "I mean, why would you even expect me to be here? I don't live in New York, remember?"

His smile was soft and his eyes intense. "Yeah. I know."

"So?"

"So Cam said you were coming over, and I wanted—"

"Yes?" She clenched her fists at her sides, forcing herself not to take a step forward, not to react at all, at least not until he said the words.

"I wanted to talk to you about the curse."

"Oh." Can a person deflate? Right then, she was certain she'd be living proof of that particular hypothesis. "What about the curse?"

"I'm, uh, doing an article—a feature piece on superstitions, that kind of stuff. And I had the idea of doing an article on your family's curse."

Suddenly, the allure of Evan was fading. She crossed her arms over her chest. "You realize I don't believe in that stuff?"

"That's why I was hoping to spend the day with you. I know Cam's story, and I know how frustrated he is with your stand—"

"Do *you* believe?"

He held his hands out to his sides. "I'm a reporter. That makes me part lawyer. I follow the evidence."

"Follow me, and all you'll get is nothing. There won't be evidence. There'll be the absence of evidence. It's not the same thing."

"We're living in Reporter World now, not Math Land. Just go with me here." He cocked his head. "Unless you don't want me to come with you."

"No!" she said, then blushed because she'd said it way too hastily. "I mean, if you want to write an article, then that's fine. I've got plans with a friend today, but—"

His quick smile lit up his face, making him seem even more delectable—and making her heart stutter in her chest. "No worries. You two go on about your day. I can be completely unobtrusive."

"Right. Sure." She drew in a breath, wishing she could reach out and touch him. And, yeah, wishing she could kick herself for sounding like such a dope. He was just a guy; she talked to guys all the time.

But he's not just a guy. He's Evan. And the idea of spending the entire day with him was enough to make the concrete streets of the city sprout with daisies and lilies and forget-me-nots.

He tilted his head, then crooked his arm for her to take. She hesitated only a second, then slid her arm through his. He was right there, only inches away, their bodies slightly touching, even if that touch was hampered by his cotton shirt and her long-sleeve T-shirt. Yet despite all that, the contact was as sensual—as soft, as arousing— as if bare skin were brushing against bare skin.

Dear Lord, she needed to stop this.

"Taxi?" he said.

She turned to look at him, still feeling off center. "What?"

"You said you were spending the day with a friend. Do we need a taxi?"

"Oh. Right. Of course." Bella's apartment was only ten minutes away by cab, and it made sense that they'd go there first, and then hit the bank branch near Bella's place so that Darcy could get some more cash.

She edged near the curb, watching Evan as he lifted his arm to hail a cab. Only half watching, really. Mostly, she was lost in the delicious fantasies about this man who'd come here today to see her.

Wonder of wonders...

And that wonder swept her forward into the street— "Darcy!"

—and right in front of a taxi that was violently swerving toward the curb.

"Darcy!" This time the scream was accompanied by a yank on her arm, and as she rocketed toward Evan, her mind processed a whirr of motion and the screech of tires. It was a blur, a mess.

And then suddenly it wasn't. Suddenly she was pressed against him. His body right there, holding her tight. His breath coming hard and fast. "Darcy. Darcy. Holy shit, Darcy, you—"

"I'm fine," she said, but she wasn't. She was shaking now, scared of what had almost happened, and overwhelmed by what was happening now. *Evan.* The way his body felt pressed tight against her. The beat of his heart, the warmth of his hands…

And the sweet tingle of anticipation that swept through her as she realized his mouth was right there, hovering just above hers.

3

TIME STOPPED AS EVAN'S heart pounded in his chest. Not from fear—he'd been terrified, but that had passed once he recognized that she was safe. And not from adrenalin, although he had a hell of a lot flowing through his veins.

Not from any of that—but from the sweet pressure of Darcy in his arms.

She was softer than he'd imagined, her curves fitting against him as intimately as if they were in bed. And, as if they were in bed, her lips were there for him, parted sweetly, red and plump and ready for his kiss.

It was enticing. Overwhelming. And he bent closer, intending to claim the prize.

She'd enticed him from the first moment he'd seen her, and each and every time he'd been with her since— at Cam's birthday parties or his wedding or any one of a dozen seemingly haphazard meetings—she'd gotten into his head. Got his blood going, his senses burning.

She made him laugh, and her analytical way of looking at the world made him think. And damned if she didn't make him hard all over, as if the effort of holding back was turning him to stone, as if he would die if she didn't touch him. Melt against him. Let her lose herself in him.

He wasn't living his life as a monk, that was for

damn sure, but it wasn't until this moment—this spontaneous press of her in his arms—that he'd truly understood why the women he dated seemed so inadequate. How could they be anything but inadequate when compared to Darcy?

He leaned closer, and saw her lips part, and for a moment he wondered if she felt it, too. If the air between them was zinging as much for her as it was for him.

He could kiss her.

Right then, right there, he knew with absolute, utter certainty that he could press his lips to hers, fold her into his arms, and lose himself utterly.

Except he couldn't.

This was *Darcy.* The woman of his fantasies, yes, but also his best friend's little sister.

And maybe that didn't matter any longer. He was a grown-up, after all, and so was she. But damned if he was going to push himself on her when she was shook up and vulnerable, in his arms only because an idiot taxi driver couldn't keep his eyes on the road.

And she *was* vulnerable. He could see it. Hell, she was staring at him with wide eyes that probably wondered what the hell he was doing holding on to her so tight now that the danger had passed.

Danger from the traffic, anyway. The danger from him? *That* still existed.

He backed away, releasing her, steadying her. "Sorry."

Her smile was like sunshine. "Don't be sorry," she said. And then she lifted herself up on her toes and kissed him.

NEVER, NEVER, NEVER would Darcy have calculated odds that would have her standing on a busy street with her arms around the one man in all the world for whom she'd held a consistent crush. And not just arms. No, there was some serious lip action going. Dreamy action. The kind of action that was making it hard for her to think, and it was when she wasn't thinking that she got nervous, because that's who she was—the girl who *thought*. The girl who calculated. Who examined the options and flowcharted the results.

This time, she'd gone with her gut.

She'd seen his eyes, and for one moment—one freakish, hopeful, wonderful moment—she'd imagined that he'd wanted her as much as she wanted him.

And for the first time in her life she hadn't thought. She'd simply reacted.

And *man, oh man, oh man* she was glad she had.

His mouth on hers tasted like ambrosia, minty and male and as hungry for her as she was for him. At first, she'd felt him stiffen, but then he'd softened, his arms going around her, his palms on her rear, pulling her toward him. She ran her fingers through his short, coarse hair, then stifled a moan as he pulled even tighter, the physical evidence that proved he was as much into the kiss as she was hard against her.

They were on a sidewalk surrounded by suits pushing past them, tourists gawking and blue-collar workers sneaking peeks as they hurried, heads down, to their jobs. And yet even though they were so blatantly on display, Darcy's body was reacting as if they were in a candlelit bedroom. And despite the fact that so far she'd had only coffee, her blood seemed to pump with alcohol, as if she'd spent hours leisurely sipping wine and staring into this man's eyes.

A curse? No way.

This was her best day yet, and that was an indisputable fact.

He pulled away, his breath hard, his face flushed. "Darcy."

She smiled.

"You shouldn't— I mean, we shouldn't—"

"Are you kidding?" she retorted with a grin. "Of course we should. You saved me, right? Doesn't that make you the hero and me the damsel in distress?"

She'd spoken lightly, but he stiffened, then took a step back, breaking the contact between them and making her insides go cold. She didn't know what had just happened, what had changed.

"Evan?"

He smiled, but it looked pasted on. "We should probably catch that cab."

"Dammit, Evan, what did I say?"

His smile wavered, and he brushed a lock of hair off her cheek. She shivered at the touch, realizing how hopeful it made her. It didn't matter; he shattered the hopes without delay.

"I just— We shouldn't."

"Why?" She wanted to kick herself for pushing, but she didn't have a choice. It was either stand and argue, or sink into tears on the sidewalk.

No way was she letting him see her cry.

"Why shouldn't we?" she repeated, forcing herself to look at him, and ignore the passersby who seemed to be there only to witness her utter mortification. And then, despite all her intentions not to lay herself out to be flayed, she heard those horrible words leave her mouth, "I thought you wanted to."

"I do," he said quickly. He drew in a breath and looked at her, the sunlight sparking the gold flecks that highlighted his brown irises. The lines of his face tightened as if he was holding something in. Then the corner of his mouth lifted almost imperceptibly, but enough to soften his expression.

"Then why not?"

"Cam," he said, though he didn't meet her eyes. "You're his little sister, Darcy."

He didn't give her any time to process *that* smack to the gut. Instead, he turned and started walking down the sidewalk, heading downtown toward Bella's apartment.

A HERO.

That was what this was—that was why she'd looked at him with such desire. Looked at him exactly the way all those girls had looked at him in high school. *No.* Not at him. At some imagined hero who'd stepped up to the plate and rescued Cameron Franklin.

What a joke.

And now the woman he'd actually wanted all those years ago had finally caught up to the punchline. But he didn't want her like that. Didn't want to be the embodiment of some childhood hero-worship fantasy.

Maybe it wasn't fair to blame backing away on Cam, but what else could he say? He didn't want her? That was a lie. He wanted her desperately. So desperately, in fact, that it was taking all of his will not to tell her he'd made a mistake and pull her into his arms again.

Dammit.

He hailed the taxi they'd tried to get earlier, and they rode in silence to Bella's apartment, Darcy shooting him the occasional confused glance. She had a crease between her brows, which appeared when she frowned.

It was there now, and he wanted to kiss it. Wanted to kiss her. Wanted to touch her and forget about Cam and play the goddammned hero if that was what she needed.

Except that he'd hated being that person in school. Hated the guilt that had filled him whenever he'd looked in those girls' eyes. Hated the fact that they were infatuated with a man who didn't really exist.

The buzz of his thoughts filled his head for the short cab ride, and he dutifully followed Darcy up the stairs to Bella's apartment.

After the rattle of locks and chains, the door opened and Bella stood there, wrapped in a fuzzy robe that matched the color of her red nose. Her eyes were swollen and bloodshot, her hair bedraggled, and her hands and pockets stuffed full of tissue.

"Don't come in," she said, her voice as thick as cotton. "I have the plague."

"Bella!" Darcy took a step forward, only to find her way blocked by the door that her friend half-closed in her face.

"Seriously, I think I'm contagious." She managed a wavering smile. "It's your stupid curse—me getting sick when you're coming into town."

"It's not my curse," Darcy said stiffly. "And if it were, *I'd* be the one who's sick." She started to reach for Bella's hand, then pulled away, knowing she'd get slapped down. "Can I get you anything? A doctor? Mass quantities of drugs?"

"We could run down to the deli," Evan added. "Chicken soup?"

"Thanks," Bella said as she turned to him. She looked like she was going to say more, but she stopped, her eyes going wide and her mouth dropping open, just a little. "Aren't you—?"

"We need to get going," Darcy said.

"No, wait," Bella said, then sneezed loudly into a tissue. "Aren't I who?"

"The guy. Evan. From that newspaper photo you have framed. The one with you and Cam after that river accident you told me about."

Darcy kept her face stoically forward, wondering if she could kill her best friend and blame it on the flu. The picture Bella referred to was from the newspaper article telling about Evan's rescue of Cam from the river. Evan been at the house, being doted on by her mother, and the local news photographer had come by. He'd snapped a shot of Darcy putting an afghan around Evan's chilled shoulders. It was the only photo of the two of them together, and since Cam was in the picture, too, she'd never felt strange about having it framed.

She'd told Bella the truth about it, though. A fact that she was now regretting.

Evan, she realized, hadn't said another word. He was looking at her with an odd expression. Like sadness. Or resignation.

"It is him," Bella pressed. "Isn't it?"

Darcy ignored Bella, opening her mouth instead to ask Evan if he was okay.

He got the words out before her, though. "Yes," he said to Bella. "That's me in the picture."

"Well, color my world," Bella said, laughing. She turned from him to Darcy. "So much for that curse, huh? You're just oozing with good luck."

Darcy bit the inside of her cheek and forced herself not to look at Evan.

"Although, maybe not so lucky after all," Bella added.

"What?" Darcy asked, alarm bells ringing. "What do you mean?"

"The tickets," Bella said. "For the show. For tonight." She licked her lips and took a step backward, as if she was preparing to slam the door against the threat of an onslaught. "I know how much we spent and how much you wanted to go, but Darcy, I can't find them anywhere."

4
_____

"HE'S GORGEOUS," BELLA said, holding a tissue over her face.

"I can't believe you lost the tickets!" Darcy was on her hands and knees, searching under Bella's bed.

"Will you forget it? I've done that." Bella blew her nose hard and flopped on the bed. "Come on. Take pity on a dying woman. Tell me what's going on."

Darcy scowled. "Nothing's going on. Except that I kissed him. And he kissed me back." She made a face.

"And—"

"And it was amazing."

Bella's brows lifted. "Either I'm sicker than I thought, or I've forgotten what the after-effects of an amazing kiss look like. Because honey, I'm not seeing the excitement."

"He blew me off," Darcy said, her throat thick. She closed her eyes, willing herself not to cry.

"Oh, sweetie. That's horrible. After all this time, and when your dream finally comes true—"

"Please. Don't rub it in."

"Did he say why?"

"That's the really horrible part. He said it was because of Cam."

"Cam?"

"Because he's my brother's best friend."

"That's it?" Bella asked.

Darcy shrugged. "That's what he said."

Bella hugged a pillow to her chest, her expression thoughtful.

"Do you believe him? Or do you think that was just an excuse because he doesn't feel the same way you do?"

Her wounded pride made her want to say yes. But the memory of that kiss made her speak honestly. "No," she said. "I think he wants me, too. I can't believe he's stepping back because of my big brother—it's not like we're in junior high any more. But what the hell am I supposed to do?"

"Force the issue," Bella said, her grin wicked.

"What? Say I don't believe him about Cam?"

"You could," Bella said. "Or you could just play on the fact that he's a man. Push until he falls, and make sure there's a mattress when he hits the ground."

"I'M SORRY ABOUT YOUR PLAY," Evan said as they maneuvered down the stairs. Darcy and Bella had spent a good half-hour tearing the apartment apart with no luck. "We could call around—maybe we could find a few seats for tonight."

She looked at him, her smile so sweet that he wanted to pull her close and hold her. "It's okay. The show's completely sold out. Besides," she added with a smile, "now I've got you for the whole evening." She took a step closer to him, making the air sizzle and his self-control falter. "Maybe you could buy me a drink later?"

"Be happy to," he said. "What do you want to do

now? Shopping? That was your original plan, right?" He wasn't thrilled with the idea of traipsing through Bloomingdales, but if that's what she wanted, he'd survive.

She tilted her head to the side, her finger pressed to her lower lip as she looked him up and down, her scan slow and deliberate. And although it was probably his imagination, he had the distinct feeling that her gaze halted—ever so briefly—at his crotch.

Whether true or not, his crotch preened under the attention, and he shifted, turning away from her and continuing down the stairs so that she wouldn't notice the way his body had decided to stand up and salute.

"Not shopping," she said, when they'd reached the foyer. "You have the look of a guy who'd rather eat nails than poke through sale racks."

"But if you want—"

"There's something I want to do more," she said, the tone of her voice making him swallow.

"Darcy..." He could barely speak through the lump in his throat, and his entire body was firing simply from the casual way she moved close to him. The tip of her nose was red, and he remembered with a sudden pang that that was the way she blushed. Not her cheeks. Her nose—and right then he wanted nothing more than to reach out and kiss it.

He forced himself not to close his eyes.

He forced himself not to groan.

He forced himself to look straight at her and pretend that he didn't want to reach out, grab her and pull her close to him.

"Don't you want to know what?" she asked.

"Huh?"

The corner of her mouth curled up, and he had the impression she was being deliberately seductive. God help him.

"What I would rather do," she clarified. "The thing I want to do more than shop."

"I…um…no. I think maybe I don't want to know."

"I think you do," she said, and before he could even draw a breath, she'd grabbed onto the front of his shirt and pulled herself toward him. Her lips pressed over his, and she kissed him, long and hard and thoroughly, and even though he knew better—even though he didn't want to be just Evan-the-Hero to her—his body, his damnable male body, sprang to attention and got with the program. Because this was Darcy, and this was what he'd wanted for so very long. Was he really so stupid or principled or *whatever,* that he was going to push her away?

No. He wasn't that much of a fool.

Or maybe he was a fool. Either way, he wasn't letting go, and as soon as his mind got to that point, his body shifted into full throttle, and he pressed tight against her, the world seeming to sparkle with sunshine and sweetness despite the shabby surroundings, the battered mailboxes and the peeling paint.

The dusty air blanketed them, crackling with a raw energy that was surrounding them and penetrating them and pressing them together. With one hand, he pulled her close at the small of her back, bringing her hips up against him, wanting her to feel his erection. Wanting her to know how much he wanted—had always wanted—her.

His other hand tangled in her curls, keeping her head firmly in the palm of his hand. She was right there, and he didn't want to let go, afraid that if he did—if he stopped kissing her or touching her—she'd disappear. Or worse, he'd find his pride again and change his mind.

Pride, however, was nothing next to the power of this woman. He'd wanted her for years. And now—false pretenses though they might be—she wanted him, too.

He was going for it.

She made a sweet, desperate noise—a cross between a moan and a cry—and the sound of it made him harder, if that were even possible. Because he recognized that sound. It was the aural representation of need, and it was washing over both of them, filling them and teasing them, the sound both a plea and a promise.

It was, however, another sound that startled him. A harsh, gutteral sound—the clearing of a male throat—and he reluctantly broke the kiss long enough to turn his head and stare up into the pockmarked face of an elderly man with kindly eyes. "You should perhaps get a room, eh? The hall, it is not so comfortable for what I think you two have in mind."

"My apartment," he said, barely able to get the words out past his need.

She nodded. "Yes."

He touched her face, then drew his thumb across her lower lip. Her mouth, once so off-limits to him, now felt familiar. Like home. Like sweetness and perfection and danger and delight all rolled up in one package.

Part of him wanted to rip off her clothes and drive himself into her, claiming her, making her his and only his.

Another part wanted nothing more than to keep this moment safe in his heart forever. He was desperately afraid that reality would come shattering around him all too soon, and he would have to face the fact that it wasn't him she wanted, but the illusion of the high-school hero. That was why she'd kept the photo, after all. Because he'd rescued her brother.

To Darcy, that made him a true hero, and damn him all to hell for not walking away despite realizing that.

But he wasn't walking. Instead, he was taking. Taking her to his apartment. Taking her in his arms.

Taking her.

Lord help him, he didn't have a choice. How could he, when his body and soul were demanding, shutting out the protests of his mind?

They caught a taxi to his place, and it jerked as the driver pulled to a stop, then rattled off the fare. They paid and got out of the cab on the proper side, thus avoiding being mowed down by traffic. No one mugged them, and Darcy didn't fall on her face while exiting the vehicle.

Neither of them tripped on slick stones or stepped in dog dirt as they entered the building.

"See?" she said, her smile wide with promise. "I told you there was nothing cursed about this day." She squeezed his hand. "In fact, I'd say it's all about good luck, just like Bella said."

Right then, he had to agree.

He pulled her close again, his hands sliding over her waist, his mouth angling over hers, and his body tightening in such a way that he knew he needed to get inside right then, or get kicked out of the building for improper conduct in the hallways.

"Inside," he said, his voice as rough as gravel as he stepped into the elevator and punched the button for the fifth floor.

"Hurry," she said, following him from the elevator to his door. The fact that she wasn't even trying to hide her desperation made him even more crazily desperate for her than he'd been half a moment before.

"I am," he said, shoving his hand into his right pocket. He frowned, then released her hand to free his left, and shoved that in deep, too.

"What?" she asked, her voice shifting from dreamy to alarmed.

"Bad luck after all," he said, slamming his palm flat against the wood of the door, his body tight with protest at the knowledge that they weren't going to be tumbling inside, tangled up with each other. Not anytime soon. "I've lost my damn keys."

DARCY PEERED THROUGH the window at the end of the hallway, looking down at the metal grating of the fire escape. No way—*no way*—was she letting something as ridiculous as being locked out destroy what she'd managed so far.

And manage it, she had. Never once would she have believed she had it in her to go after a man the way she had, but this was Evan, the man she'd wanted beyond all others. Once she saw it in his eyes—once she knew that at least a little, he wanted her, too—she found the courage to do what needed to be done, despite Cam, despite curses, despite Evan's own loyalty to the fraternal boys' order of best friends.

She was a seductress, she thought with a smile. Only this seductress was currently without a place to seduce, and that simply wouldn't do.

The fire escape looked solid enough. But it also

looked entirely unconnected to the interlocking pieces of scaffoldlike grating that formed the fire escape leading from the various apartments. "How are we supposed to get from here to your place?" It was an important question. Because right then, she wanted nothing more than to be inside his apartment. Specifically, she wanted to be inside his bedroom. And barring that, she might just have to jump him on the fire escape.

Frankly, that iron grating didn't look all that comfortable…

He squeezed in beside her, his proximity making her feel warm and gooey, and she realized that she was smiling. *This* was luck. Heck, it was more than luck—it was perfection. The one man she'd wanted for as long as she could remember, and she was actually going to have him. In bed. Soon.

Hopefully.

She frowned at the fire escape. "Maybe we should go to a hotel," she suggested.

"It's a thought," he said. "But we're here, and odds are good my window's not locked."

He climbed past her onto the grating, then held out a hand to help her. She followed eagerly, slowing only when she felt a tug near her butt and heard the distinctive *rrrriiiiipppp* of tearing denim.

"Nail," she said.

His grin flashed. "There you go. More evidence of bad luck for my article."

She crossed her arms and looked down her nose at him, making her expression purposefully haughty. "Is that a fact? I'd think you'd see it as good news." She turned so that her rear was aimed at him, then bent over a bit so the material stretched, opening the newly created hole and revealing the elastic leg-hole of her panty and the curve of her butt. "After all, it's one more way into my pants."

The air between them sizzled. "Darcy?" he said, his voice rough.

"Yeah?"

"We need to get into my apartment. Now."

Her breath shook as she tried to steady herself. "There?" she said, nodding at the grating to her left, about three feet over and a few feet higher than the grating on which they stood. "That's it," he said. "Easy."

She glanced at the concrete ledge that protruded from the building, then watched as he stepped onto a milk crate someone had left on the fire escape as a seat. He stepped onto the ledge, held on to a steel pin that protruded from the brick and took one long step over to his own fire escape landing.

He was right. It looked damn easy.

"As soon as you're on the ledge," he said, "I can take your hand."

"Right. No problem."

She was wearing black boots with a narrow heel—she'd splurged on them since she'd thought she'd be going to the theater—and she had to admit they weren't the best for scaling buildings. But she was only going up and over—not any more involved than climbing a set of stairs.

After a quick mental pep talk, she climbed onto the milk crate, then lifted her left leg to the ledge.

"Other leg," he said. "You're facing the wrong direction."

"Oh."

She hadn't been paying attention, but now that she

looked, she saw what he meant. "No problem." She tried to turn, got her heel caught on an indentation in the ledge, felt the heel break, and then caught that protruding steel bar in the nick of time as her body went sliding off the ledge. Evan's shout filling the air.

"Evan!" She realized she was screaming, but wasn't the least bit embarrassed about it. Dangling five floors above the apartment courtyard was plenty scream-worthy.

She didn't, however, have to scream for long. Because just as she was wondering how on earth she was going to manage to hang on to that tiny little steel rod, Evan's warm arm wrapped around her.

"I've got you," he said. He was clutching tight to his fire escape with one hand, while the other held her tight. "I won't ever let go," he added, and she believed him. More than anyone in her life, she believed that he'd always be there to catch her.

With his help, she managed to get back onto the ledge, regain her balance, then cross over to him. Throughout all of that, she kept her composure. But as soon as they were on his landing—as soon as her feet were on solid ground—she clung to him. Not in tears. Not in terror. But in the urgent, desperate need to show him exactly how she felt about him. To demonstrate with her body how she would give everything to him, just like he'd promised everything to her with those five simple words.

"Open the window or break the glass," she said. "Now."

Fortunately for the super of Evan's building, the window was unlocked. And since that was so damn convenient, she didn't chastise him for what was a really stupid habit. Instead, she slid her hands over his chest, pushing him backward at the same time onto his bed, gratified to see that the fire escape had opened into the one room she most wanted to be in.

"Thank God," Evan said, his fingers snared in the cotton of her shirt as he tugged it up and over her head. It stuck there for a moment, and he laughed as she struggled. But those struggles ceased when his hands cupped her breasts, pushing her bra up and freeing her flesh. His hands snaked to her back, and he unfastened the clasp, then tugged her free of the bra. At first she felt only the brush of his thumb over her nipples, each in turn. Then his hands disappeared and she, desperate to know what he was doing, attempted again to pull the shirt off her head.

She paused as she felt his mouth close over her breast, his tongue flicking her nipple even as his hand roamed the flesh of her belly, easing down until his fingers were dancing over the button of her jeans.

She couldn't move, much less get herself free, and she arched her back, moaning, finally thrust back into action by the desperate desire to touch him the same way he was touching her.

With one solid yank, she tossed the shirt aside. His gaze was focused on her, his face pressed against the soft swell of her body, but he looked up, and his eyes said it all. This time, she watched him as she moaned.

"Evan," she whispered, then slid her hands over his back. He still wore clothes, and that was unacceptable. With a laugh, she took hold of him by the shoulders, then rolled him over, the motion freeing her breast from his mouth. The air that rushed against her damp flesh made her tremble, not from a chill, but from the promise of what she knew was to come.

"Hey," he said, as she pushed him flat onto the bed, then eased herself over to straddle him.

"Hey yourself." His fingers had done their work on her jeans—the button was open and the zipper down. Now those same nimble fingers slid inside, tight between the denim and her crotch and the silk of her panties, moving with deliberate purpose over her soaking wet panties toward her clit.

She eased her hips up, ostensibly part of her movement to kiss him, but also to give him better access, then moaned as his finger slipped over her core, the sensation no less erotic because his hand was outside her panties.

In a bold movement, she pressed her mouth to his, claiming his, her hands on his shirt, her fingers fumbling at the buttons. With her tongue, she explored his mouth, learning the way he tasted, the way he responded, wanting to consume him and be consumed by him.

When she came up for air, she realized she hadn't made progress on the shirt. "Damn," she whispered.

"Really?" he said, raising an amused eyebrow.

"How much do you like this shirt?"

"At the moment, I'm feeling less than charitable toward it," he admitted.

"Good." She grabbed the sides and ripped it open, sacrificing a decent shirt and the flying buttons for the pleasure of quickly accessing his body.

His chest was warm with a smattering of hair, and she splayed her palms over him, her eyes closed as she explored with her hands and then with her mouth. His own hands were still exploring, and as her tongue flicked over his erect nipple, she shifted her hips, silently urging him to peel off her jeans.

He got the message, and his fingers left her sex long enough to grip the material at her hips and tug.

It wasn't a maneuver that could be finished with her straddling him, her mouth on his chest, and apparently he realized that. She gasped as he flipped her over, then mimicked her position, with her straddling him, and his hands tugging and pulling until she was free of both jeans and panties.

"You, too," she demanded, gratified when he nimbly and quickly stripped. "If you say you have no condoms in this apartment, then I'll admit to my entire family that I believe in the curse of the Franklins."

"I wouldn't dream of being the cause of weakening your convictions," he said with a smile, then leaned to the left and tugged open a bedside table. She mentally applauded, but let him handle the sheathing himself— her fingers were shaking too much in anticipation.

But *oh, sweet heaven* it was worth the wait. His fingers stroked her first, and as he did, she clutched his back, her fingernails digging into his flesh, her mind wiped of any thought except pleasure—giving and receiving.

"No more," she said, desperate for him to be inside her. "Now, dammit, before I go completely crazy."

"As you wish," he said, his eyes twinkling. She was so wet that her body opened easily, accommodating him, and she lifted her hips to urge him further, deeper.

He thrust against her, and she mimicked his motion, their bodies coming together in an ancient, primal, horizontal dance that had her soul coming loose from her body, borne away by the pleasure of it all.

His face was red with effort, and he held tight to the headboard as he ravaged her, causing the bed to rise and fall with their movements. She watched, meeting the growing pleasure inside her, and saw his jaw clench as his own release drew near. Her breath was shallow now, matching his, and then, as their bodies merged to one, they both went over the edge together, their low cries full of satisfaction.

"Dear Lord," he said, then collapsed beside her on the bed, which bounced a bit in response, then seemed to shift beneath her.

"Evan?" she asked, startled. "What is that?"

"What?" he asked, dreamily, but she didn't have to explain herself or ask again. The cause of the shift became clearly apparent when, with a loud *crack*, one side of the bed collapsed, sending them tumbling to the ground.

5

"WE BROKE YOUR BED," Darcy said, looking completely mortified as she sat up from where they were now tangled naked on the floor. "Evan, it's an antique. It's probably worth something."

"Not anymore," he said, then chuckled at the pained expression on her face. He took her hand and squeezed. "I swear, it's fine. It's an old bed, but it's not of great value. I promise. And I'd been thinking about buying a new one anyway. Something bigger, like a king."

"You don't need to," she said, her expression almost shy, which under the circumstances seemed a little strange.

"No? Why not?"

She swallowed, then met his eyes. "Because I'm totally keen on snuggling close when I come into town to see you."

"Oh." Her words eased through him like warm brandy, and he fought the urge to lean in and kiss her. Not because he wanted to fight it, but because he knew he had to.

"Evan?" Her voice was quick. Alarmed.

He focused on a point over her shoulder. "This was amazing, Darcy. *You're* amazing. I've thought so for years." He swallowed, not quite believing what he was actually about to say. "But I don't think we should…"

He trailed off, not sure of the words. But she just stared at him, her mouth hanging open and her eyes shining with the threat of tears. "Oh, God, Darcy, I'm sorry. It's not you. It's me."

That earned him a crooked smile. "Never thought I'd see the day when a reporter pulled out such an old cliché."

"It's not a cliché when it's true," he said. He took a deep breath for courage. "Darcy, I'm not the man you think I am."

Her brows rose, and she laughed. "Who do I think you are? Daniel Craig?"

He couldn't even crack a smile. "I'm not a hero, Darcy. It's all a lie. A stupid, foolish lie that made everyone think I was a guy that I wasn't."

He waited, expecting her to speak, but she didn't.

"That newspaper article you keep in your bedroom?" he prompted. "It's a lie. Dammit, Darcy, don't you get it? You've had this fantasy of me for years, but I'm not that guy."

"Evan—"

He held up a hand. "*No.* I'm not that guy," he repeated. "I didn't rescue Cam. Hell, I helped him get into that mess in the first place. But we couldn't say anything because your mom would have a cow, so we made up the story about him falling off the bridge, and—" He shook his head. "It doesn't matter. The point is the whole town thought I was a hero, but I hadn't done a damn thing. I'm not that guy," he repeated. "But what I am is a guy who has wanted you since the first time I saw you. Who thinks you're fascinating and smart and funny. A guy who now knows that the reality of having you was even better than the fantasy." He reached out and brushed her cheek. "But Darcy, I don't want fantasy with you, and I damn sure don't want to *be* a fantasy."

"You're not," she said.

"No, I mean it."

She laughed. "So do I." She reached over and took his hand. "I know. I've known for years."

That, he wasn't expecting.

"How?"

"Cam, of course. He knew I had a huge crush on you. He said there was no way you'd be interested in a freshman, but after the whole river fiasco, he told me the truth. I guess even though you weren't interested in a freshman, he figured I still wanted to know everything about you." She shrugged. "The truth was, it made you even more of a hero to me."

He lifted his brows. "Why on earth would you say that?"

"You kept a secret. A huge one that was important to Cam. That's what heroes do, right? Protect their friends."

His laugh shook through him. "Darcy, sweetheart, you're amazing."

She dragged her teeth over her lower lip and cast a playful glance at the crooked mattress. "Want to show me once again just how amazing you can be?"

"You only have to ask," he said, then drew her close, his body firing again, ready to take her and claim her once and for all, the primal need to make her his almost overwhelming him as much as the heady certainty that she already was.

This time they moved more slowly, though, savoring each other, exploring and teasing, tasting and tempting. He reached blindly up with one hand and groped for a pillow that had tumbled onto the floor along with them. He put it under her head, then kissed her hard. Then he reached for another pillow and put it under her hips, lifting her to exactly where he wanted her.

"Evan." Her voice was soft, dreamy, and he heard it despite the rustle of skin against his ears, the soft skin of her inner thigh to be exact, which pressed against him as her body arched up, her moans and cries and soft passionate noises making him even harder than the taste of her already had.

He licked her slickness, then added his finger to the mix, stretching her wide, wanting nothing more than to be inside her, and when he couldn't stand it anymore, he eased up, kissed her with her own taste still lingering on his lips, and drove himself home.

Heaven, he thought, and she repeated the thought in words after the storm passed and she lay clinging to him. "It feels like heaven."

"We can stay here all day," he said. "Your brother would be happy. After all, I'm keeping you safe."

A few hours later, he'd made her that much safer, and they both lay exhausted on the carpet. This time, her skin glowed rosy from the setting sun.

"You'd be catching dinner now with Bella," he said.

"I like this better," she said, speaking the absolute truth. This had been the most perfect day of her life, which pretty much disproved that whole curse thing as far as she was concerned. "Right now, the only thing I'm hungry for is you. Somehow, I just can't get enough."

"But you did miss the play," he said. "I'm sorry about that. Why don't we try to get tickets for next weekend?"

She laughed. "I'll be right here next weekend, but we

won't be going to the theater." She pressed a kiss to his bare chest.

The high-pitched tones of her cell phone startled them both, and she grabbed it up, then answered, listening at Bella's rapid-fire words. "Thanks," she said with a grin to Evan. "Feel better soon."

"Bella?"

"She said she hopes we're having fun, and if we're not too worn out from our busy day, that we might want to go to the theater tonight."

"Sorry. Not following you."

"She remembered that she never even had the tickets," Darcy explained. "They're waiting for me right now at the will call window."

She leaned forward and settled purposefully beside his naked body. "See?" she said, leaning in and brushing her lips over his. "Nothing but good luck today." She nipped his lower lip. "But frankly, I don't think I'm in the mood for a show after all."

* * * * *

DEVON'S DILEMMA
Kathleen O'Reilly

1

April 1, two years earlier

THE EAR-SPLITTING NOISE of the alarm clock was sadistic and cruel, and most hellishly of all—four freaking hours too early. Devon Franklin rolled over again and threw the covers over her head.

Three o'clock in the morning.

For a moment, there was blessed ignorance. The idea that she had accidentally missed the alarm, or that she had suffered a temporary brain spasm. Unfortunately, none of those things were even remotely close to being true.

The digital watch was within easy reach on her bedside table, but she knew the date. The other three hundred and sixty-four days of the year she woke up with a sigh of relief, because it wasn't...

April 1.

Bone-tired and furious, she succumbed to a fit of juvenile rage, and slammed her hand over the off button, silencing the beep and hopefully killing the clock in the process.

April Fools'. Ha. If she were an average twenty-eight-year-old female, with a life expectancy of 78.1 years, nonsmoker, healthy diet, within ten pounds of

her ideal weight, she could blame the crack-of-dawn
buzzer on a no-good-sibling prank, or a moronic friend
getting carried away with a holiday that was nobody's
idea of fun.

However, she was a Franklin.

Cursed. People thought curses were cute and funny,
and only happened to pretty people. Oh, yeah. If only
that were the case.

Being the most rational Franklin, she knew the safest
path to a relatively pain-free day. Hibernate in bed until
midnight and wait the disasters out. It was what the rest
of her family called Devon's Ostrich Solution.

She hated when they said that. Maybe it wasn't the
most daring (Cam), optimistic (Darcy) or academic
(Reg) strategy. However, it remained an undisputed
fact that of the four siblings, Devon had a lower inci-
dence of medical traumas. From an early age, as soon
as she understood the eventful complications of the
Franklin curse, Devon had hunkered down and opted
for maximum protection against whatever bad things
came on April First. Sure, it meant that her life wasn't
nearly as lively...

Oh, boo hoo hoo.

Now she'd done it. Completely debated herself into
wakefulness when she wanted nothing more than to
sleep. Devon sunk down farther into the blankets,
waiting for the sounds of silence to wash over her and
hopefully deliver her back into the sleepy arms of
Morpheus, who was the only man who dared come near
her on April Fools'. Yes, that was what she was doomed
to for her sex life. Imaginary Greek gods.

Instead of sleepy silence, hard rain rapped like coins

on the old roof of her tiny cottage, quaintly set in the middle of Middle America.

Maxbass, North Dakota. Nothing ever happened here. Devon had picked the town three years ago for that reason.

She craved nothingness. She ached for nothingness. A booming blast of thunder scoffed at her nothingness, rattling the double-paned, tornado-proofed, hurricane-secure windows.

Outside, another sound mixed with the rain. An unsettling dragging sound and some sort of howling. Not quite an animal. But it could be an animal. A bear. A lion. A zombie. In Devon's mind, all were highly probable.

From outside the house, the moaning noises continued, but there was absolutely no way she would investigate. Nope, she would bury her head under the duvet and live out the next twenty-four hours in blissful ostrich-buried-head-in-the-sand-I-know-nothing mode.

But what if it was something bad? asked that incessant voice inside her head.

The doorbell rang, and Devon lifted the comforter away from her face, opening one cautious eye. On the wall opposite her bed, the bank of security monitors showed an empty doorstep, with a dark shadow hovering just beyond the porch. An intruder?

Statistically, in a town with a population of four hundred and thirty-seven, intruders or burglars were unlikely. As her wretched inquisitiveness began to take hold, though, she lowered the covers another inch. Over the years she had learned that no matter how she tried, problems didn't go away when you ignored them, they merely smashed through windows (April 1, 2000), or roofs (April 1, 1982), or drove through the living room (April 1, 1993).

But Devon was more determined than most of her family. She'd finally wised up and had pimped out her tidy two-room cottage into a modified nuclear bunker, outfitted with a state-of-the-art monitor and surveillance system, all nooks and crannies visible from every room, and best of all, fashionably accentuated in a cheery yellow.

Each room contained a row of screens that displayed a live feed of all the other rooms in the house, including the exterior perimeter. If disaster was going to strike, Devon wanted to know in advance.

The ordinary citizen would consider the elaborate setup overkill. However, the ordinary citizen would have suffered a psychotic breakdown from the streak of April firsts that she'd had.

Devon, never a dummy, had learned.

The doorbell rang, and this time the shadow was fully visible on the monitor. Not Morpheus, no, this was a man. Human, living, breathing, and looking almost…sane.

His dark T-shirt clung to a brawny chest, and flexing arm muscles were artfully displayed as he leaned on her doorframe.

Thanks to the rain, his dark hair was plastered like a skullcap to a nicely formed head, and in spite of the weather, he seem calm and fairly controlled. The overhang of her porch wasn't doing much to keep him out of the storm. A wave of drops washed over his face, and he dragged a hand through his slicked hair, pushing it away from his face.

A magnificent face. Chiseled and thin, with a dimpled chin and a mouth that looked as tasty as ice cream, maybe tastier. His eyes were the best feature. Pale underneath black brows and spiked black lashes, they gleamed as if he were actually enjoying himself.

Although it was 3:00 a.m. on April Fools' Day, Devon's lady parts were especially wide awake.

For a few dazzling seconds she stared as the rain sluiced over his face, along the broad shelf of his shoulders. It was like watching a guy in one of those soap commercials, those devious marketing ploys where the product was for a male, but the target audience were women who would be goggle-eyed over a bare-chested young man relishing his sensual time alone in the shower.

Her legs twitched and she realized the inherent dangers of this situation.

Aroused or not, she wasn't stupid enough to actually answer the door.

As if sensing her momentary weakness, the doorbell rang again, the monitor showing a determined bent to the man's jaw, as if he knew someone was home, and through evil, sexy-man, mind-control powers could lure her to respond to his call.

Not in this lifetime, buddy. Pick another sap.

Devon pulled the duvet over her head because she could be more stubborn than anybody, anytime.

The doorbell rang again.

And again.

And again.

This time, he left his finger on the bell, one long, very annoying ring that echoed behind her eyes like a hangover, or tinnitus, or an annoying stranger who thought foolish people should open their doors at 3:00 a.m.

Whatever.

The doorbell rang again, and that was it. Devon threw back the covers, and flipped on the light switch next to her bed. Without missing a beat, she grabbed the flashlight that was strapped to her bedpost, stuffed her feet into her slippers (after first checking for spiders) and then trudged to the front door. Not that she was going to open the door. Yet.

From the bank of monitors in the living room, she could see more. The Air Force squadron insignia on the T-shirt, complete with wings. The base wasn't that far. The man was a pilot?

Damn it. Did he have to be in the Air Force? Devon could ignore pushy Girl Scouts and their cookies, she could ignore Facebook friend requests for weeks and she shooed away stray animals that might possibly mistake her home for something other than the small pit of hell that it became on April first every year. There'd been one small cat, but that was a tragic story best left alone. After suffering through an endless saga of disasters and hoaxes, Devon was immune to everything.

The man peered into her camera. Correction: Devon was immune to *almost* everything.

In spite of the familiar feelings of foreboding, ignoring a 3:00 a.m. doorbell-wakeup call by a member of the U.S. Armed Services, well, it seemed…un-American.

Or at least that was what her lady parts were telling her.

Cautiously she unlocked the three dead bolts, although the security chain stayed firmly in place. After the door creaked open a scant three inches, Devon warned, "You should know that my boyfriend is a black-belt instructor, and also a cop, and he's got a loaded shotgun aimed right at your privates. So make it good and make it fast, because he's not happy and someday you might want to reproduce, in which case you'll need your jewels intact."

"Howdy, ma'am. Sorry to bother you and your boyfriend. I know it's late, but I need to borrow a phone. You see, there was this bachelor party. I'm ashamed to admit it's sort of blurry, but I need to call and get a ride back to the base, and I can't find my cell."

His drawling voice was rumbly and slurred, an odd combination that spoke of both sexiness and irresponsible drunken stupor, neither of which Devon approved of, but both of which stirred irresponsible sexy shivers inside her.

Knowing the road to high insurance premiums was paved with shivers exactly like this, she managed a mocking laugh.

"Oh, come on. Do you think I'm stupid enough to open my door to a drunken stranger at 3:00 a.m.?"

"Well, of course, if you were alone, I wouldn't expect you to let me inside. I can hear that clipped no-nonsense tone in your voice. Very sensible and smart, 'cause God knows there's a lot of kooks in the world. I had a grandmother that sounded a lot like you, and she hailed from West Texas, and could shoot down a coyote and then serve it up in a stew. I have yet to meet anybody more practical than that. Until now. But it seems to me that as long as your boyfriend isn't itchy on the trigger, I'll make a quick call, and be home before I drown. Seems to me we'd all come out alive, and you and your man could content yourself with the knowledge that you helped a forlorn human being in his dark time of trouble."

Realizing she'd been outfoxed by a tipsy man, Devon rested her forehead against the door. She didn't want to do this. It just reeked of…Devon ending up with the short end of some pointed and painful stick. Knowing she was doing the smart thing, her hand pushed the door shut.

Right before the door was securely latched once again, the miserable man sighed, a melodramatic exaggeration of both starving orphans and homeless kittens that might have melted a softer heart.

Devon's fingers hesitated, keeping the door open only a hairbreadth.

"Look, I'm sorry about this," he explained in that raw voice that stroked down her increasingly wobbly spine. "If it wasn't raining, I'd wait it out, but I'm soaked and my leg hurts—"

"What did you do to your leg?" Devon asked, flipping on the porch light and then opening the door before stepping back in shock.

No way did the tiny three-inch image on the monitor compare to the sucker punch of the full in-person effect. His hair wasn't merely black, it was the startling blue-black of stealth bombers, gun barrels and every other doomsday device known to man. Long thick lashes framed silvery gray eyes, which were currently wearing that ah-shit look that she knew well from having two older brothers, who, not being nearly as accepting of their fate as Devon, experienced ah-shit moments on what was a nearly daily basis.

Her mouth went dry from looking at him, and in her mind, she was already calculating the estimated maximum loss if she just did something small, like touch him, like kiss him, like seduce him.

Oh, for Pete's sake, what was she thinking? Instantly she made a note to get a bigger vibrator.

Devon locked her arms across her chest, determined to remain unmoved, uninvolved, unaroused and alive.

"The leg's not injured. It's uh…encumbered," he answered, those silver eyes widening innocently, which should have been impossible, considering the slightly tipsy tilt to his mouth…and the ball and chain around his leg.

Ball and chain?

Devon slammed the door shut.

2

"Owwww!"

That wasn't a good sign.

Devon cracked the door open again. "Did I hurt you?"

"Just the nose," he muttered.

"Sorry," she apologized, then added in the spirit of total deniability: "Please take a step back before it gets beat up again." All legal waivers of liability completed, she slammed the door shut. If his nose got out of joint this time, it wasn't her fault. He'd been warned.

Seemingly incapable of showing good sense, he knocked quietly.

"Ma'am?"

Her eyes closed, as if a lack of vision could block out the insidious persistence of that voice. This man wasn't used to women who slammed doors on his nose. He wasn't used to horrible miseries for one day of the year. No, he was that clueless individual who believed that all mountains should be climbed and all plumbing leaks could be fixed with a wrench and a roll of duct tape.

In other words, he was a man.

If only he wasn't so…tempting.

After suffering from previous April Fools' day hoaxes that required FBI interrogations (no she wasn't a terrorist, and she didn't know any Nigerian princes, nor had she ever claimed to be one) and accidents that required interior fumigation, it was somehow freeing to know that she wouldn't mind spending twenty-four hours in bed, if Mr. Ball-and-Chain were there to keep her company.

Sensing her defenses starting to falter, Devon moved to the offensive. "Do not attempt to guilt me into opening the door against my better judgment, knowing that you're an escaped criminal with a sordid past, recently on the run from a chain gang."

"No chain gangs in North Dakota, ma'am. The penal system is a lot more humane than it used to be. No, this is just my buds pulling an April Fools' joke on me."

An April Fools' joke? Seriously? For the first time on this godforsaken day, she found herself actually smiling. "You have very sick friends."

"I know, I tell them that every day. You don't know how many times I wanted to ditch the bastards, but then I tell myself, Self, you'll get shot down behind enemy lines and captured, and if I went and kicked their ass— exactly like they deserved, mind you—then they'd have no reason to pull off one of those death-defying rescues you see in Hollywood and I'd never get famous. So you can see, I don't have any choice in the matter. And that's why I'm here at your doorstep with a ball and chain wrapped around my leg. It's pitiful. It's pathetic. But you're my last hope. And I know you're a very smart lady, and shouldn't open the door, but goddamn it, it's cold and wet out here, and the base is sixty-five kilometers away and I think if I was one hundred percent sober, I could probably make it, even with this monstrosity attached to me. But currently I'm sitting at about seventy-eight percent sobriety, and I think I'm coming down with a cold." He sneezed, a genuine sound that breached the nuclear-bunkered walls of her heart.

All biological dictates aside, Devon knew there were a thousand reasons she shouldn't open the door. More importantly, no self-respecting female would let a slightly drunken voice curl her toes and cause her spine to collapse upon itself.

But something about that low, hot summer drawl made her warm in places that had forgotten they could get warm. Her skin was starting to feel tight and itchy, and she had a strange desire to dig through her lingerie drawer to find something more attractive than a red-rose flannel gown. All further arguments against the door opening died a short and violent death.

Maybe it was April Fools'. Maybe it was a mistake. But so what? As a female, more than eighty percent of her decisions that involved the male sex would be a mistake. As an actuary who calculated life and death expectancies on a daily basis, Devon believed in always playing the odds.

After she opened the door, the first thing she noticed was the blood that trailed down from the bridge of his nose, and meandered along his cheek. It was a nice cheek, innocent and undeserving of blood caused by her. Automatically she reached for the first-aid kit on the wooden cabinet nearby, and then handed him an antiseptic wipe and a piece of gauze.

She hoped he'd had all his shots. Yes, her front door was made of steel, and tetanus shouldn't be a problem, but Devon wouldn't be surprised if a rusty nail hadn't winged its way to her home sometime in the last few hours.

The man wiped away the blood and then waved a casual hand. "No problem. No boyfriend?" he asked, and she noticed the steady watchfulness in his gaze. *Not as tipsy as she had thought.*

"I have an alarm system," she answered, pointing to the big red button. "It's very good. One wrong move, and you will be eviscerated."

"I assure you, there are no evisceration plans in my future. I'm fingerprinted and on file with the U.S. Air Force, and they'll mostly vouch for my sterling character, although don't ask about last Halloween and the colonel. He's still a little touchy. Right now, I just need to use the phone, and then I'll be…" Gazing down at his leg, he winced, and then pulled at the chain with one powerful hand, creating that fingernails-on-the-chalkboard dragging noise that she'd heard earlier.

The noise was almost worth the visual. While she watched his strong movements, thigh muscles bulking underneath faded jeans, biceps enlarging and then elongating with each tug of the chain, tension featured on his face much like a man in the throes of…

of…

of…

…orgasm. Yes, *orgasm* was what they called it.

A momentary twinge of nostalgia started in her brain and then settled happily between her thighs.

The heavy black ball left tread marks on the linoleum. Permanent tread marks that would be impossible to clean up. Still, linoleum could be replaced, and frankly, Devon was currently enjoying these twinges. Later, there would be some sort of penance, but her insurance (home, life, car, flood, travel) was paid.

"Are you getting married?" she asked, the cultural implications of a ball and chain just sinking in.

He looked at her, horror in his eyes, and then seemed to pick up on her thoughts. "Not me. I'm not that stupid. The ball and chain was for the groom. It was my idea, but I got double-crossed. Damned tequila."

Her mouth twitched, nearly curved into a smile. What a dilemma, and here was a man who defied gravity in million-dollar flying machines designed to protect his country and the lives of innocent citizens the world over.

In Devon's opinion, *hero* was merely another word for fool.

And yet he was also a man who took his pranks seriously, but when outpranked, took it in stride. Refreshing.

She schooled her features into something not quite so admiring. "And you got chained up instead?"

"Bastards," he answered with a grin. "Retribution will be sweet, swift, using methods unsanctioned by the CIA. Phone?" His deliberate gaze took in her small, tidy, kitchen, took in her small, tidy house, but she noticed how carefully his eyes did not take in the small, tidiness of *her*.

She was accustomed to it and had settled into a peaceful acceptance of her solitary existence. Was she pretty? Yes. Was she worthy of a flirty wink or a cat-call? Yes. Was she worthy of risking a car off the cliff or a seemingly demonic attack dog? Not a chance in hell.

Calamities such as what she termed the Cujo incident—sometimes in the presence of the opposite sex—were why her evening attire was a thigh-length flannel nightgown (flame-retardant), why her brown hair was tied back in a very practical long braid (she was too vain to cut it off), why wool socks had a hole in the right toe (currently hidden by the skid-proof slippers), why he wasn't hitting on her…

"The phone's over there," she muttered, pointing toward the old princess-style phone with a frankly cranky finger.

Up until this moment, she'd considered herself above the superficiality of the eternal quest for male companionship. It worried her that now, in the presence of a lustworthy serviceman tied to a ball and chain, she might be devolving—condemning herself to a life of women's magazines, drawers full of mascara, cottage cheese and, worst of all, *exercise*. Seventy-eight percent of all weight lost came back on. Exercise was futile, it was painful. In the end, Cujo was preferable.

"I won't be long," he said apologetically, most likely noticing the sour expression on her face, which she should erase. But if she did, then wasn't she falling into the very trap that she wanted to avoid?

He picked up her pink receiver and then promptly frowned.

"I'm not getting a dial tone," he said, as if surprised.

Devon shrugged, perhaps a bit cocky. "Sometimes that happens with storms," she replied vaguely.

"Damned phone companies. Never there when you need them most. Do you have a cell?"

Seeing the easy confidence in his expression, Devon's smile became more sure. "Absolutely. Do you want to try it?" Not that it was going to matter. She'd bet the last dollar in her emergency savings account (well-funded) that there was no cell reception. No, Mr. Who-Needs-Insurance was going to be stuck.

Alone with her.

At that lusty thought, she almost grinned. Instead, she handed him the sturdy mobile phone that she kept for emergencies.

Efficiently he punched in numbers, holding it up to his ear, and then nodding, as if there was an actual chance in hell of communication with the outside world.

Devon waited.

Disaster in three…two…one…

Still confident in a rational world order, he started to talk. "Scott, it's Chance. Yes, Chance Cooper, your squadron commander, the one currently toting an extra fifty pounds, you son of a bitch. Your ass is mine, Airman."

He kept grinning, talking successfully, actually arranging car pickups, meeting places, time synchronization without any thought to contingency plans. And most remarkable of all, the phone connection was still working. The overhead lights still were shining brightly, there were no strange animals or people jumping through her windows.

It was…ordinary. Immediately Devon sensed there was something wrong with this world. Maybe it wasn't April 1. Maybe time had frozen, or sped up, or shifted to a parallel dimension. A new and unfamiliar twinge of emotion sprang up inside her. Was this a feeble spark of something that might could be termed hope?

And oh, yes, look outside the window—flying pigs, no less.

Once again secure in her own well-protected lifestyle choices, Devon rocked back on her slippered heels and prepared for impending disaster. Blissfully ignorant,

Chance continued talking while secretly she ogled him and his sodden, dripping, drenching hunk of body.

Her eyes lingered on the black T-shirt that clung to his well-hewn arms. On that bulky chest that might have attracted a more shallow female. She knew those military types believed in physical fitness, and she told herself it was logical that such athletic musculature would cause her tongue to cleave to the roof of her mouth.

Proof that the man was human was a small scar above his right eye, nearly concealed by the thick curl of black hair. The scar was a neon sign that perhaps he wasn't quite as lucky as he believed. Devon liked it, the way it spoke of hard-fought battles, as if his waterlogged attire and slightly swollen nose weren't enough. But oddly, it was the tiny scar that kept tempting her eyes.

Survival. That was what it stood for. The scar told of disasters surmounted, and wounds that were healed. He carried no provisions for emergencies. He simply persevered.

Fascinating.

And exactly why had this unlikely specimen of oozing testosterone showed up in her house tonight?

Just as she was contemplating the slim, statistically unlikely, struck-by-lightning, lottery-winning long shot that he might have brought something good into her home, the man stopped his cheerful chattering and swore.

"Phone died?" she asked, blinking innocently, as if she didn't know.

"It must have been the battery," he muttered, and right then the bank of overhead bulbs began to spark, pinging one after another like targets in an arcade game.

Devon exhaled with relief. There was an odd comfort to her survivalist existence, and she didn't like change. When she was a young and naive twenty-one, she'd been tempted to believe that the curse wouldn't affect her life. That she should go balls-out like her brothers, Cam or Reg. After four bad breakups, long nights alone with Ben & Jerry's and a lot of movie rentals, Devon realized that balls-out was for idiots who actually enjoyed emotional pain.

Exactly on schedule, her backup generator kicked in with its comfortable hum, illuminating the room in an eerie yellow glow. Chance looked at her with surprise and respect, not quite so life-zestful anymore.

It was about time. If things had stayed the way they were—communication working, electrical facilities intact, fuel gauges functioning—she might have been lulled into complacency. But Devon knew that history repeated itself. The statistics never lied. "Are they coming to get you?"

"We got cut off before I could give Scott the address. If he were more resourceful, maybe he'd reason it out, but God bless him, he's not the brightest tool. We usually just call him Tool, in fact."

"I think you're stuck," she announced, folding her arms over her chest, and his amused gaze drifted lower, touching on the perfectly adequate curve of her breasts. It was as if he could see through her crossed arms, see through the heavy flannel, see through every bullet-proof (literally) defense she had ever designed.

A perilous tingle slid down her body, a tingle that had nothing to do with temperature, and her nipples tightened into buds.

Seeing the very visible proof of her discomfort, he smiled, a cocky, pilot's smile accustomed to wrangling gravity and seducing women while weighted down with a ball and chain. Prudently Devon reminded herself that there was no insurance policy on her vagina.

"Do you have a car?" he asked.

"No," she lied because she never drove on April 1. Ever. Even if the insurance company allowed it, she wouldn't.

"What about the Ford that's parked in the garage?"

"I don't have a Ford in the garage," she lied.

Chance pointed to the keys that hung on the hook next to the door, and the big keyring labelled "FORD".

"That sure does look like car keys to me, hanging right there next to the door, exactly where any person with a lick of brains would put them. My ex-girlfriend, she was always losing her keys, and I told her that she should rig up something like that so she wouldn't forget. We broke up because I just couldn't handle dating a bubblehead. You don't look like a bubblehead. Now, I understand that you wouldn't want to go out in this weather. Hell, neither would I, but that would leave me here, dripping all over your very clean living room, coating this newly waxed floor with water and muddy ooze, and you don't look like a woman who's comfortable with ooze."

"I wouldn't have to be comfortable with the ooze if you sat outside all night," she explained.

"Or alternatively, why don't you drive me home?" he asked, in that sweetly, coaxing voice as if she were some brainless female that would roll over and play "America's Next Ho" at his command.

It was a testament to his physical appeal that both possibilities were not out of the question.

"I'm not driving in the storm," she insisted, shoring up the remainder of her defenses.

"Then, as you said, I'm stuck," he told her, leaning back against the wall, completely at ease in the unfamiliar surroundings. His hands were jammed deep in his pockets, the prototypical male pose designed to accentuate the male package. As if she would fall for such a primitive ritual designed to show off a man's mating prowess. She would not look, would not look.

Devon looked.

At the sight of the large denim-encased bulge, Devon swallowed, and something swollen and throbbing thrust inside her. An unbidden fantasy of sex with this man and his…swollen, throbbing sex.

Outside, while the elements raged, a tree branch crashed against the window, shaking the unbreakable glass. The branch was an ominous sign, reminding her of the last time she'd had sex on April Fools' Day. Peter Hollowell had ended up with a bee sting on his privates. A swollen and throbbing bee sting.

Devon pushed all thoughts of sex aside and collapsed into the nearest chair. "Do you want to sit down?"

"I don't want to drip all over your furniture."

"I use Scotchgard."

"Still, I can stand," he answered, completely nonplussed, breathing completely even, the broad planes of his chest falling up and down. The soaked fabric clung like a second skin, lovingly caressing the hard textures of his body.

Her fingers curled into fists. Tight, non-caressing

fists. "I have some sweats you could probably wear. My brother's. If you want something dry." *Something that wasn't quite so...stimulating.*

He raised his right leg. "I don't think I could get anything past this without divine intervention."

"A hacksaw would do the trick. I have one."

His mouth drifted to a lazy grin, an easygoing expression that didn't quite make it to his eyes. "A hacksaw? Who are you? Some sort of engineer?"

"I'm an actuary," she replied. "But I believe in tools." Locks without keys were pretty common in her experience. From there, a hacksaw seemed like a no-brainer.

He looked skeptical, but didn't call her a liar. "As long as your hand's steady, I'm willing to give it a go."

3

CHANCE WAITED. By now, the tequila had worn off, and he was stuck with an extra weight on his leg, and an extra six inches in his shorts.

Holy shit. Who would have thought it?

The woman—Devon Franklin was what her Stanford University diploma said—had prepared for any and all emergencies. He'd only met one other woman who'd stocked a hacksaw, and after he'd discovered her fondness for Spanish Inquisition-style torture, he'd understood why. Leather and steel just didn't fire his juices. He liked bare, sweaty skin against his chest, big squishy globes of female sexuality that made him happy to be a man.

Devon Franklin had globes. No, they weren't big and squishy, but those weren't mosquito bites, either. His mind wandered, pondering the exact size, color, shape and palm fit of her globes, and before he knew it, his mind had her naked and panting, and…

Whoa.

He shifted in his jeans, wearing a hard-on that no amount of denim was going to hide. Maybe he wasn't in such a hurry to get back to the base after all.

Out of the corner of his eye, he saw movement and

he wheeled around, but it was only the security monitors on her wall. *Only.*

Was she in witness protection? Doubtful. Little Miss Devon Franklin was nobody's fool. She would have taken down whoever was out to get her first.

While he was contemplating her don't-tread-on-me personality, conflicted with the sultry mysteries of her body, he noticed her image flickering on the tiny screen. It probably wouldn't be right to spy, but they were her security monitors, and she was aware they were there, and what was he going to do? Glue his eyeballs shut?

Right. His conscience now free, he watched as she dug into her closet, neatly putting aside an eye-popping array of tools.

Actuary and engineer, since a hardware store sure as hell didn't have that many tools. One by one she pulled out a hammer, two sets of wrenches—metric and standard, three pairs of safety goggles, a crowbar and a vibrator.

He kept his laugh low, starting to like this Devon Franklin, ever practical, ever prepared.

She put the saw on the bed and then sauntered over to her bedroom mirror. Her hands moved to the long braid that trailed down her back. It surprised him how badly he wanted to see that silky fall of hair framing her sweet face.

Silently he prayed. His breath caught, waiting to see if she was going to let it loose.

But then she scowled at her reflection and the braid stayed in place. Chance shook his head, disappointed with her. Still, she wasn't immune to him, the night was young and it wasn't as if Scott was going to come roaring to the rescue. No, for the moment, Chance and Devon were all alone.

"Got it," she called as she entered the room, holding the saw like a trophy. As she moved toward him, he watched her walk, watched the easy sway of her hips. Not showy, but purposeful. He'd bet everything that she did was purposeful. Having sex, for instance.

Realizing that he was drifting a little too far and a little too often down into the dank gutter of carnal delights, Chance told himself to throttle back. But then she stood opposite him, hacksaw in hand, in that old-lady nightgown that revealed exactly nothing, and his stubborn mind started undressing her all over again.

Unaware of his debauched thoughts, she glanced at him, glanced at the saw, then glanced at the heavy chain around his ankle. "I think you should sit down."

If he sat down, there was no way in hell she'd miss the hard-on. "I don't want to mess up your house," he said, because honestly, she was a very nice lady, and he'd feel a lot more comfortable if she was staring at his ankle, rather than his crotch.

"Please. I can't do this while you're looming."

"No one ever called me a loomer before," he said, but now he was resigned to defeat. He had tried to stay a gentleman, she had rebuffed his attempts and he had no choice but to willingly go along with whatever things she had in store.

He sat, his legs splayed to give her plenty of cutting room, because that was one big-ass cutting instrument. Sure, she looked competent and efficient, but he wasn't taking any chances.

She sank to the floor, wedged between his knees, creating even more pornographic images that were cheap and sordid and completely undeserving of such a capable young lady, who'd been nothing but gracious—except for the nose job, but hell, he couldn't really blame her for that one.

Soft and capable hands shoved up the hem of his jeans and grasped him around the bare calf. Honest to God, it was better than porn.

Chance grabbed the wooden chair arm for support, and tried to ignore the firm feel of her fingers on his bare skin. She took the saw, poised it over the chain and her hands moved back and forth with a slow, steady, rhythmic movement.

"You need any help?" he asked, trying to be polite, trying to ignore the way her neckline gaped only slightly below the two unfastened buttons at the top. Or the way a dark vee promised great treasures to whoever delved farther below. Never shy about exploring, he leaned over, angling a little farther, until she pushed him back with a firm hand to the thigh.

"You need to sit still," she ordered, in that firm, husky voice that was some cross between schoolmarm and nightclub singer.

"It's going to be a lot of work to cut through that steel. I just don't want you to exert yourself too hard on my account."

She rested the saw on the chain and shot him an intense look. "Do you want this off?"

"I'd love to get it off, ma'am," he answered sincerely. She blushed, and he was a no-good scoundrel for teasing her, but he liked to see her blush, her cheeks pink, her brown eyes dancing with life. "If it's not too much trouble."

"Sit still," she ordered.

"Maybe if you could sort of brace against my leg for

moral support. It's a little unnerving, the size of that blade, and I'm very attached to my leg."

She leveled him with a flat stare. But to his eternal happiness, she scooted closer, her chest resting mere inches from his knee. Not shy at all, Chance moved his leg, closing the distance, gratified to feel the soft cradle of her bosoms warm against him.

She glared, and he shrugged innocently. "You don't mind, do you? It's sort of comforting."

She muttered something which could have been "whore dog" but no matter, because she didn't move. He sat there quietly, his life in her hands, while she sawed at the chain. The gentle weight of her breasts brushed against him, back and forth, and he watched her work, the dark line of her lashes, the way she bit her lip with concentration. When the chain refused to budge, she scooted closer, pulled up the hem of her gown, locking her legs around his one, using his weight for leverage. Chance had always loved physics, but never so much as now.

With each stroke, the teeth of the saw cut deeper into the metal, and she moved closer, too, her gown inching up higher, exposing nicely toned legs. Starting to realize that he wasn't nearly as much in control of his emotions as he wanted to believe, Chance shifted uncomfortably and she stilled her sawing.

"I won't be held responsible if I amputate your foot."

"I'm doing my best," he apologized. "It's not every day I sit through this, and your legs are starting to distract me. You got some very adequate muscles there, not too hard, not too soft. I dated a biker once— Schwinn, not Harley—and she had these rock-hard calves, like somebody injected a steel paperweight under her skin, and sometimes when she'd be rolling around...well, we don't need to go there, but yours are a lot nicer. Firm, but they don't feel like office furniture."

"I suppose you broke up with her, too," she muttered.

"Actually, she found religion and felt like I was a sinful influence, so she told me that it was best that we didn't see each other anymore."

Two months later, the female in question had called him at 3:00 a.m., well and truly plastered and ready to denounce all her newly found principles of the more celibate lifestyle, but Chance didn't feel like that bit of information was germane to the conversation.

"You don't look very heart-broken," she told him.

"No, ma'am. I like my women soft. More—" he gestured with an innocent hand "—pliable."

She didn't answer, but went back to sawing, although he noticed that she was working it with a lot more force than before. This woman had some seriously untapped energy that was just begging to be tapped. Honestly, she'd be a lot less tense if she gave herself over to a willing man, which was one of those bullshit justifications that men use when they know they have no business thinking what they're thinking, but Chance tried to be honest with himself. He knew his flaws, and he took responsibility for them.

Next thing he knew, the steel link broke in two, and the chain rattled to the floor, the ball rolling free. He'd still have a leg iron around his ankle, but he could live with that one. At least he didn't have to drag that damned cannonball around anymore.

Now that her work was done, Devon moved back,

and tucked her gown demurely around her ankles, breaking his heart in the process. The view of those legs had been mighty nice. In fact, the only nicer view would be legs spread, locked around his back, squeezing around him....

Chance snapped out of the fantasy and noticed her curious look. "Thank you for doing that," he told her politely, sincerely, and without a trace of "I think we should get naked" in his voice.

"No problem. Let me get you those dry sweats."

When she moved to rise, Chance offered her a hand, taking a little too long to let go. Once again, she looked at him curiously, appraisingly, not the impatient go-to-hell sort of glares he was getting earlier. She probably didn't realize that her mouth was slightly open, her eyes slightly darker, and he didn't feel it was in his best interest to point out either feature to her. But he noticed. Something was changing....

As she walked from the other room, his mind was full of sinful ideas that should have shamed a more gentlemanly man. But Chance had a full appreciation for the biological desires and habits that had been preordained when man had arisen from the primordial ooze with his cock fully erect.

He liked Devon Franklin. She wasn't his usual pornolicious bedmate, but she intrigued him. Not many women were that cynical and hard-nosed, but still wore flowery flannel. He ached to know what was underneath all that flannel, and undercover recon of the female form was what Chance Cooper did best.

He was happily pondering his path to seduction when a long rumble of thunder shook the house, rattling the foundation and sending the cannonball rolling across the floor.

Where it landed on top of his foot.

Considering the impurity of his thoughts, Chance thought it was no more than he deserved.

4

ONCE SHE WAS SAFELY IN HER BEDROOM, Devon collapsed on the four-poster, and exhaled a breath she didn't know she'd been keeping. The house shook, not that she was worried; the specially reinforced concrete foundation was built to withstand 400 PSF.

If she truly played the odds, she would retrieve a pair of sweats, get Chance Cooper safely clothed and then kick him out of her house so that she could experience the rest of this day in easy disassociative peace, where nothing bad could intrude.

But right then, she didn't want peace—or not that kind of peace. She wanted a piece of Chance. He was darling, and sexy, and the sort of womanizing Casanova that she needn't feel guilty in case he got stung by a bee…or some other mildly poisonous insect. He was a man who could take care of himself.

A man who could take care of her.

She closed her eyes, imagining those hands on her, and her heart raced in double time, constricting the flow of oxygen to her brain, causing her to sigh, a breathy, exhilarated sound, often signifying delight.

On April Fools', how often did she get to sigh with delight instead of defeat? Not once.

Hadn't she earned this? She'd seen the liquid heat in those clever eyes. All she had to do was say the word, and he'd be on her like gasoline on dying coals.

But how to seduce a man like that? She wasn't Bubbles McBimbo with come-on lines that rolled off her tongue. Her underwear drawer consisted of exactly one thong, a present from a short-lived boyfriend, that had EAT ME on it. Not the image she wanted to present. Not to Chance. Not today.

She contemplated the monitor, the ever vigilant, all-seeing eye, and then smiled to herself. Security had its price, but security had its pleasures, too.

Could she do this? Of course.

Her mind made up, she moved to the screen on the wall, pushed the button to display the living room camera and then retrieved her brother's old sweats from the drawer. If things went according to plan, Chance wouldn't be needing those. For a few greedy seconds, she imagined him, and a flash of lust shot right between her thighs. She could imagine his hard body primed and waiting for her; all she had to do was put on a show. Painfully aware of the camera in the room, she watched herself in the mirror as her hand went to the top button on her gown, flicking it open.

Out of the corner of her eye, she could see the video feed from the living room, and sure enough, there was Chance, focused on the image of her. The sharp look of need on his face gave her all the encouragement she needed; she flicked another button open, and then two.

Her palms slid beneath the fabric, cupping her breasts, and she tilted her head back, feeling the growing desire guiding her actions.

Her body began to sway, not like dancing, that would be too obvious. No, this was the simple hip-curling movements that spoke of a woman who was in the throes of sexual arousal.

Her breasts felt heavy and swollen under her hands, her senses heightened to near breaking, and she pushed her gown off one shoulder, exposing a tight nipple to cold, biting air and she gasped.

On her monitor, she could see him standing alongside the tiny screen. His back was to her, and she wished she could see the expression on his face, but all she saw were the rigid cords in his neck, the steely line of his shoulders and the firm muscles in his back straining against his thin T-shirt. Although her sampling of men wasn't as large as she would have liked, and most of her dates ran to the disastrous, Devon knew an aroused man when she saw one.

Slowly she freed her other shoulder, sliding it from the nightgown, until the warm comfort of the old flannel was shoved to the floor.

Devon Franklin was bare to the waist.

In the carved mirror above the dresser, she could see the powerful lust in her eyes, her lids falling heavy. All her muscles turned soft, except for one, the low, hammering pulse between her legs, the one that was directing her movements in spite of the risk.

Her brain knew that all pleasure came with pain, but this time, it was a statistical certainty that whatever the pain, the pleasure would be greater.

Her hand slid over her breasts, down the relatively firm line of her torso, gliding further down beneath the yellow cotton panties. Her legs moved apart, and she braced her free hand against the dresser top, taking a deep breath, toying and teasing. She didn't dare check the monitor, she didn't dare know what was happening to Chance because she was so turned on, she didn't want to know the hard chill of rejection. She didn't want to think about falling tree limbs, or wrong phone numbers, or magically misplaced keys.

No. Today, she was going to live.

Daringly, she slid one finger inside her, feeling the wet, swollen flesh, and Devon sighed with relief. Oh, yes. Oh, please, *yes*. Her fingers moved, knowing the places that gave her pleasure, recognizing the building of pressure, the fluttering clenching and relaxing of muscles. Lost in this magical world, her hips rocked back and forth.

She could only think of her black-haired stranger with starkly pale eyes. She gazed into the mirror, met those pale eyes and her whole body froze.

He was here.

This was no longer safe solo sex on a screen. This was full-body contact, this was sweat and skin…with a high probability of never sleeping with Chance Cooper again.

Devon swallowed, sliding the wet-slicked finger out of her body, and lodging it safely behind her back.

One side of his mouth quirked upward with an easy tenderness. She liked that about him, the way he simply accepted things and moved forward.

His fearless intent, the hard strength of his body and his easy confidence flew in the face of every deterministic model that Devon had ever devised. She started to shake—nerves, emotions and the certainty that she didn't want to be alone with her fantasies.

"I thought you might need some help," he told her. Silvery eyes raked over her bare breasts, admiring her, desiring her. "You'd been gone so long that I wasn't sure if something was wrong, or you might have been in trouble and—oh, hell, honey, I aced high-G training and breezed through bat-turns and I have never been this knotted up before."

His voice was hoarse and unsteady, missing the easy charm his tone held earlier.

"Can you stay?" she asked, dangerous words that sounded foreign on her lips.

He didn't answer, but limped toward her, his gaze locked with hers. She loved the fire in his eyes; hypnotized her. Tonight she wanted the burn.

She thought he would touch, ached for him to touch her body, but he didn't. Instead, his hand reached for the braid at the back of her head, capturing the length of it, tugging ever so slightly.

"I want to see your hair down. I want to see it splayed over your shoulders, long and silky. It's beautiful and you keep it hidden in plain sight." His free hand touched the tip of her breast lightly, short-circuiting her nerves, blowing all function to her brain. "Like these."

Sadly she possessed no backup generator for her mind.

"Can I take down your hair?" he asked. The request robbed her of words, of any survival technique. Devon nodded once.

Gently his hands pulled and discarded the elastic band. Patiently he took apart the braid, one section falling, then another, fanning it out over her back, over her shoulders. She shivered from the warm feel of his hands in her hair, skimming over her skin, and from the sensual brush of the strands.

Devon never wore her hair loose. It was impractical and silly, and she'd told herself a gazillion times that she should cut it off if she wasn't going to do anything with it, but now she knew why she'd refused to cut it. Because she was waiting for the one man who knew. The one man who was willing to work his way into her tightly braided hair and, in the process, make her feel gorgeous, admired, loved—instead of cursed.

The way he looked at her now, as if there was no other woman he ever desired more, she didn't feel cursed. His nose was starting to bruise along one side, at some point, he'd developed a limp, but he was still more amazing than any other man she'd ever met.

Maybe it was an illusion. The ultimate April Fools' joke. Maybe he was a good actor. Maybe, maybe, maybe. For one night though, Devon wanted to go with maybe.

5

CHANCE TANGLED one hand through the heavy fall of her hair, wondering what fool had invented a braid. It was an instrument of torture to deprive mankind of something this...lovely.

Her hair was the color of the Badlands in the afternoon sun: sand and fire and light and shadows. And soft like silk over his fingers.

His thumb pressed against her lower lip, watching the dazed awareness in her warm brown eyes, feeling the raging want inside him, and he struggled to keep the brakes on, because this one was different.

Oh, sure, he needed to kiss her, he ached to kiss her, and his cock was ready for long past kissing, but he wasn't sure how to start, or where to start. He'd seen lots of naked women, and as a rule, tits, mouths and legs didn't throw him off...until now.

But holy shit, she, of the Rapunzel hair, of the Craftsman toolbox, of the gorgeous breasts...

He was saved from puzzling out exactly how to first touch Devon Franklin because those breasts were soon pressed shamelessly against him. She kissed his mouth, and stole his breath. Chance wrapped his arms around her, trying not to break her, trying not to damage her with the metal on his ankle, but his hands weren't as gentle as he wanted them to be.

The long line of her spine, the soft pleasure of her skin, and oh, hell…the hot brand of her nipples against his chest.

His hands slipped lower, curved his palms around her ass, pushing her into him. Sweet heaven, his cock honed between her legs like it were custom-made to be there.

Not that she seemed to notice. Her fingers dug into his damp T-shirt, yanked it over his head and then she curled her arms around his neck, kissing him once again. Hot damn, the woman could kiss. Her mouth was greedy and hungry, as if she hadn't gotten laid in eighty years, and Chance didn't understand what was wrong with the men of this no-account town because if he lived here, he'd be all over her, two, three, ten times a day.

He wanted to climb inside her, those soft pliable legs curving around him…his cock jerked enthusiastically and he knew that was a bad sign. If her tongue wasn't quite so erotic, creating these colorful pictures of him inside her, surrounding him, her body moving just as erotically as her tongue….

Needing to throttle back to somewhere in-control, Chance broke free from the kiss, took a step back, letting his attention wander to her breasts, which had intrigued him since pretty much the first time she opened the door.

For a woman of such a practical mind, she had exceptional breasts, rounded and glowing rosy. Fascinated, he brushed his thumbs across the twin peaks, and Devon shuddered, her dazed face a picture of woman-in-want. It was a glorious look, her normally lucid eyes staring at him as if he were the only man in the world.

It was an awe-inspiring responsibility. Determined to live up to her high expectations, he lowered his head, and took one nipple into his mouth, drawing long and hard, until her hands tangled in his hair. She began to whisper things to him. Words such as *liability* and *sustainability* and *binders* and *survivorship,* which on their own would have bored him to tears, but when coupled with sexual organs nearly cooked his munitions right then and there.

His jeans and jockeys were shucked in world-record time, and he dragged her back to him, ready to…

No, he told himself.

"Devon," he whispered, "honey, we're going to have to slow down if you're to have an enjoyable experience with this. As a man, I'm pretty well guaranteed to hit the brass ring, but if you don't—"

She pushed him down on her bed, rising over him, and the dim light cast golden shadows on her and her dark hair falling around her.

Her eyes were so sexy and sleepy, and he watched her teeth worry her lip. Doubt, concern. Obviously, she was not a woman who gave herself up to the carnal side of life. He had expected that, but hadn't fully expected the incredible emotional distress that his cock currently was experiencing at the idea that she might worry herself to the point of stopping this.

"Is there something wrong?"

"I should warn you."

Oh, those were vile words. Disappointment struck at his heart, his gut, and other vital organs. She was married. That had to be it. There were ethical, moral lines that he did not cross, and he was rather proud of his more honorable nature. But to be fair, he'd never had a nearly naked married woman straddling his completely naked body and what had been firm, uncrossable lines, now seemed a little shortsighted. His conscience warred with his cock, and his conscience won.

"You don't need to warn me. *Warn* is a strong word, implying bad things, but let's cover all the bases, so we're clear. Are you married? Engaged? Is your heart spoken for? Do you have some disease that I should be more concerned about than I currently am? Are you taking some drug that makes you uninhibited and thus are not in full control of your senses? I think those are all of the circumstances that could discourage me from having intimate relations. So if any of those are applicable, a simple yes or no would be appreciated."

"No," she answered, and he began to breathe again.

Until he noticed the teeth still working her lower lip in a busy manner that shouldn't arouse, but did. "I can see you've still got some questions."

"What about you?"

"I'm footloose, disease-free, got a couple of parking tickets in Fargo and someday they'll catch up with me, but that's it." His eyes widened at his own thoughtlessness. "Condom! And by the way, I have that…in case you don't."

Considering the provisions in her house, he would bet his right nut that she had a condom, too.

"I have a condom," she confirmed, but she didn't sound enthused. Goddamn it. He had liked her enthused.

"Why don't you tell me what the problem is? I can't fix it, unless you talk about it." To be honest, he could lay here all night, with those no-nonsense legs astride him, damp panties rubbing his belly like some X-rated good luck charm.

"It's not that easy," she told him, sad and forlorn, and he reached up, brushing his thumb over her mouth to make her smile again.

"I know I don't look like a man of intelligence. People think I'm just some pretty flyboy who's a few noodles short of a casserole, but you should know that I graduated pretty high up in my class at A&M. I *can* fix a lot of things. Why don't you try me?"

"I don't believe in duct tape. It's a cheap fix that wouldn't withstand a real crisis, and if I'm going to do something, I should commit one hundred percent, not try to bandage it up with a patch that won't last in the long run."

He started to laugh. "Is this a survey on home repair or sexual proclivities?"

"It's a metaphor," she said, sounding miffed.

"For what?"

"My life."

Damn. Whenever women started talking in broad, nonsensical strokes that involved the words *my life* or *my feelings,* it didn't bode well for relaxed conversation, for sex, or for effective communication between males and females. However, he was interested in hearing her philosophies on life because he suspected it wouldn't involve body image or shopping, or the evils of panty hose. No, he instinctively knew that Devon Franklin worried about things on a more serious plane.

So, despite the screaming protest of his cock, Chance pulled her down on top of him, burying her head in his shoulder, and rubbed her back. Up and down, his long comforting strokes might put him in mind of the sexual act, but his heart was actually in the right place. Hopefully she would overlook the heat-seeking missile that was jutting impatiently against her belly.

"What's wrong?" he asked, just as the yellow lights of the generator dimmed, glowed and then diminished to black.

"That."

"I like the dark," he said against her hair.

"I'm cursed. You should know that most men who sleep with me end up running in the opposite direction as fast as their feet can carry them, which usually isn't very fast, because they get beat up, or attacked by wild dogs, or caught up in a terrorist sting, or chained to strange devices and I don't mean that in a sexual way. I mean bad. Cursed. Bad."

"Listen, darling, I think you're probably being overly dramatic. My track record isn't that hot, but you don't see me throwing in the towel. A sexy woman in the prime years of her life—that's you—should not be creating obstacles to your future physical happiness. There's no such thing as curses."

"It's real. Your ball and chain. Your nose. The power, the phones."

She sounded so woebegone, so convinced that everything was her fault. It was refreshing to find a female who wasn't quick to blame the male species, but in this case, he felt guilty because none of this was her fault.

"Devon, I made the ball and chain as a joke. I grabbed a cannonball from the base and bribed a grease monkey out of his welding gear. And if you bumped my nose, that's only 'cause I'm stubborn and don't take rejection easily. Not that it happens often, which is why I'm unfamiliar with exactly how to handle it. But if you think you're to blame for any of my stupidity, well, that's just stupid."

She sniffed and smiled and pressed a kiss to his mouth. A soft kiss that willed him back into sexy thoughts again, not that they had been far away.

"You're very nice," she whispered, and it touched him in multiple places—his mind, his heart, and his cock, as well, which went without saying, which was why he felt the need to correct her.

"Not that nice. Let me tell you the sordid truth about men, sweetheart. You lie naked against them, sexual fulfillment so close that their minds are already imagining it, then they will tell you anything to get into your pants."

"So you didn't mean all that?"

"Of course I did, but that doesn't mean I don't want to get into your pants."

"I wish you would," she said softly, sliding one bare thigh between his two willing ones. Chance dug his fingers into the sheets because although the unmistakable moisture between her legs said yes, he could still hear the worry in her voice. In his opinion, if a woman wasn't fully committed to the task at hand, then his duty as a first-class lover had failed.

"In case you haven't noticed, we're already 99.9% to liftoff, sweetheart. I don't know why .01% would stop you now."

She lifted her head and he could feel her stare, hear the relief in her voice. "We are, aren't we?"

"Don't think I've ever been this close without sealing the deal before," he offered, pleased to see his words were helping. He'd never had a woman tax his mental skills before, and it was kind of fun.

"You seem very unafraid."

"I might be quaking inside, but I give you my word, I do my best work under pressure."

For one moment, she was silent, and he thought his well-honed instincts might have been off, but then her hands reached down and she stripped off her panties. The nightstand drawer squeaked open, and Chance sighed with relief. Sure, he would have tried to seduce her out of that small yet significant piece of cotton, but his conscience rested easy now that she was the one who'd made the final move.

"If something bad happens," she started, and he pressed his mouth over hers, squeezed himself into the condom and then pushed inside her.

"Oh," she breathed, and he loved that soft sound, that quiet hitch in her breathing. Something soft and quiet whispered inside him, yet he froze because his world was the ground-shaking roar of Pratt & Whitney engines, the shrieking sound of sirens and reveille at dawn. Against all those booms and rattles, Chance had forgotten what calm was like.

But then her muscles clenched around him, firm and demanding, and he drove into her, deep and hard.

6

THERE WAS THUNDER and some sort of shattering explosion, but Devon didn't care. All she wanted was to stay here in bed, over Chance, under Chance, submerged in mindless bliss.

Her nails raked over his back, his sculpted ass. Her mind knew her house was going to collapse, but she needed this. She deserved this.

After all, it was April Fools' and she was having the very best sex of her life. Her back arched in ecstasy, and she felt the harsh bristle of his jaw against her neck, most likely drawing blood, and before the first orgasm passed, the second one began.

Her mouth flew open, trying to form words, a scream, a prayer, and the buzz of the alarm clock brayed in her ears. Chance threw it against the wall, hitting the mirror.

Breaking it.

Over and over he thrust inside her, the old wooden bed no match for what was apparently a lifetime of unexplored passion. First there was a crack, then a thud, and finally a splintering sound that meant disaster.

Right as the bed frame collapsed, Chance rolled them to one side just as they crashed to the floor. He took the brunt of the fall, one quiet oomph. Before she could call 9-1-1, he was filling her again.

Certain that this was her last, best sexual experience ever, she rained desperate kisses over his sweat-damp neck, the hard planes of his chest, willing him to stay, in case her thighs padlocked around him weren't a big enough hint.

But somewhere in her mind, it dawned on her that he wasn't running, he wasn't leaving, he wasn't even slowing down.

The unbreakable window shattered, shards of glass flying, but he picked her up and ran to the living room before she was hit.

"How you doing?" he asked, climbing on top of her, busy hands on her chest, and she loved the sound of his unruffled drawl.

"I told you I was cursed."

He kissed her mouth, her neck, the tip of her breast, and she didn't feel cursed. Quietly she sighed, a breathy, exhilarated sound that definitely indicated delight.

"And I told you I do my best work under pressure. Lay back and relax, honey. The night is young, and I want to hear all that dirty actuarial talk again. Assuming, of course, that the roof doesn't fall in," he added, tempting the fates.

Thankfully, he had her safely in the basement before it did.

7

DEVON AWOKE to the unfamiliar sensation of a brawny arm thrown casually across her breast. The basement floor was hard and cold, and her body protested as she began to move.

A new day. April 2. Ah, yes, she thought, steeling herself for what was to come. Rejection day. Normally it didn't hurt this much.

"Good morning," he told her, sitting up and rubbing his dark hair, and looking too darn cheerful to reject her. Sometimes men could be pigs. Sexually virile pigs with finely honed bodies, but pigs nonetheless.

"I hope you're not hungry," he continued in that same cheery tone, "'cause I don't think there's much left of the kitchen."

Then he leaned over and kissed her. Soft and lazy, and very unpiglike, and some of the steely walls of her heart started to melt. It was the nicest thing any man had ever said to her on the morning of April 2. Actually, it was the only thing any man had ever said to her on the morning of April 2.

"I suppose you'll want to get back to the base," she began cautiously, since this was uncharted ground.

"If you feel up to driving. You seemed sort of skittish

before. Or, if the phone's working, I can call Scott if it's too much trouble." Slowly he rose, uncurling his long length, and Devon felt another punch of lust as her gaze drooled over him.

"No. Let me get dressed," she said, keeping her voice just as light and carefree as his. Carefully she picked her way up the basement stairs, into the remains of her house and sighed.

It was worse than usual, and she wanted to cry. Most of the walls had been blown in, the floor was a collection of dirt, unbreakable glass, drywall and mud. Quietly, Chance came to stand behind her, and to her surprise, he wrapped his arms around her, as if this were some ordinary morning.

"Looks like a tornado came through. I'd like to think it was my earth-shattering sexual prowess, but you don't look gullible enough to fall for that one."

Her mouth curved up, and in the face of destruction and desolation, she smiled. She was insured. "A one-house destruction zone is more like it."

He pressed a kiss against her neck, and against her rear she could feel the thick length of his sexual prowess growing again. "Let me dig out my jeans and stow away the heavy artillery before you think I'm completely un-civilized. Then I'll help you clean up."

"You don't have to," she told him, stepping away from the warm safety of his arms. She picked up a throw and wrapped it around her. Men never stayed. They never helped, and certainly Chance was more well-mannered than most, but she was a Franklin.

The endings never changed.

The sunlight drifted in from the east, tracing over

him, and he was so perfect, so beautiful, so out of her league, but she had a lot of nice memories. It was going to be easier next year. Even alone. She could sit on her couch, eating ice cream until the power blew, and remember the one perfect night with Chance Cooper.

Quickly she wiped at her eye and sniffed. "There's a lot of dust in the air."

His lazy grin was back in place, and he tilted up her chin. "Honey, I know I don't have to. But this looks like a hell of a lot of work, and unless I get my ass in gear, I'm going to miss my dinner date."

His dinner date? She swallowed the boulder that was lodged in her throat because that was the April Fools' joke. Finally, she understood. Despite what he'd told her earlier, he was involved, or married, or engaged. "No, we couldn't have that."

She tried to pull away, but he kept her close, and then, adding insult to injury, reached under the plaid blanket and patted her ass. "I hope you like steak. After last night, I could use the protein."

His hand lingered, wandered, but Devon was no longer insulted or downhearted. Actually, she was starting to feel…happy. "I like steak, but it's hard on the heart."

"Devon, there's nothing harder on the heart than you are. I'll take my chances with steak."

Devon couldn't help it. She kissed him.

"So are you this much fun on April 2?" he asked, a long moment later.

"Not nearly."

He blew out a relieved whistle, and his glinting silvery eyes made her quiver all over again. She could see this might be an ongoing problem.

"I gotta tell you, that's a real relief. I know I told you I do my best work under pressure, but I underestimated the full extent of your libido. I couldn't do this every day." His fingers trailed down her spine, the completely unneeded throw falling to the floor.

"Every other day of the year, I'm actually very boring," she told him quite primly. As primly as a naked woman could.

He looked her over, once, twice, and took her back into his arms. "Boring? You? Not a chance."

"You're okay with this? It's my life. Actually, it's my entire family's life. It's this curse. Once a year, things just go bad."

He pressed a soft kiss on her forehead. "Not so bad. In fact, some parts of last evening were so exponentially-not-that-bad the word *curse* just seems wrong."

She didn't understand. She kept throwing him these opportunities to leave, but he acted as if he wasn't going anywhere. "You're willing to go through this again? In the future?"

"This?" he asked, raising a brow. "Honey, I'm Air Force. Any Task. Any Place. Anywhere."

Ruefully, she shook her head. "I think I'm going to like you."

"Think? Think? You're blowing holes through my considerable ego with these doubts. What do I have to do to convince you?"

"I got ideas," she said, pressing against him quite shamefully.

He began to laugh, found a nearly destroyed cushion from the couch and they fell on it together.

"Yup," he whispered, covering her mouth. "Yesterday was my lucky day."

It was some time before Devon could think about those words, but when she did, she knew. Yesterday was her lucky day, too.

* * * * *

REG'S RESCUE
Julie Kenner

1

April Fools' Day, one year ago

"FOLKS, THIS IS CAPTAIN Edwards. We've been dodging several severe weather cells, and control has instructed us that we won't be landing in New Orleans as scheduled. Instead, we're being diverted to Houston. We apologize for the delay and we'll get everyone to your final destination just as soon as we can."

A collective groan rose up from the passengers of flight 1281. Professor Reginald Franklin didn't groan, but he did turn and look at his watch, his movements stiff and forced.

Maybe they'd still make it in time....

He hoped to hell they'd still make it in time....

He closed his eyes and gripped the arm rest, thankful he'd decided to cash in his air miles for first class. Because, frankly, he needed another drink, and he took his hand off the armrest long enough to press the call button.

He'd been traveling now for almost twenty-four hours, having left Oxford less than an hour after he'd received Jean Michel's e-mail. He hadn't talked to the antiques dealer in years, but now his old friend had said he'd found something—something important. Something Reg had given up searching for.

Something that might lead to ending this curse.

Reg hated traveling on such short notice, but he couldn't risk taking the time to pack or plan. He needed to be on the ground on April 1. A Franklin at thirty thousand feet on April Fools' Day was a bad idea—his brother Cam's formerly reckless life had proven that.

Not that Reg's planning had done any good. He'd arranged everything so carefully to ensure that he was safely on the ground well before 11:59 p.m. on March 31. He hadn't, however, accounted for the weather. And now it looked like they'd be arriving into Houston in the wee hours of April 1.

He clutched the armrest tighter and hoped they didn't crash. For the most part, the curse was personal. Surely his presence wouldn't bring down—and injure or kill— an entire plane load of people?

A pretty, blond flight attendant with a brilliant white smile leaned over and clicked off his call light. "What can I get for you?"

"Scotch," he said.

Her smile widened. "Rough flight?"

"The delay's not helping."

"We're so sorry about that."

"Nothing you can do," he said, feeling the futile weight of fate pressing down on him.

"I can get you that drink," she said, and headed off to do that. She returned momentarily with two tiny bottles and a fresh glass with ice. She winked at him. "I thought you could use a double."

"You thought right." He opened one of the bottles, poured it over ice and drank it down, feeling the Scotch burn his throat and numb his body. Good. If he was still in the air at midnight, he wanted to be numb.

There was no one seated beside him, and he leaned over to peer out the window at the scattered lights below. The clouds blocked most of the view to the ground, and the night further disguised their location. He assumed they were over Louisiana and moving now toward Texas, but he didn't know for certain, which gave him room to imagine that they were in fact passing over their original destination—New Orleans.

She was down there.

Anne.

The thought sat like a stone in his gut, the simple knowledge that he would soon be physically closer to her than he had been in years.

Emotionally, though…

Well, they'd broken those ties three years ago.

He pulled away from the window, his motions feeling suddenly jerky. As a professor of archeology, he'd ostensibly taken the position at Oxford in order to be closer to the excavations on which his academic pursuits had focused. But the job had also been a symbol, a statement. There was no denying that much, especially not to himself. And the statement had said simply that he was abandoning his nonacademic research; that he was giving up the hunt for clues about how to turn off his family curse. He was moving on, letting it lie.

Being done with it and everything about it.

He hadn't regretted the decision. His quest to end the curse had brought him almost as much misery as the curse itself.

Ruefully, he rubbed his thigh and the long, ragged

scar that still ached in bad weather even though it had been thirteen years since the April first on which he'd tripped over a piling at a dig site and ripped the hell out of his leg on a steel post that had reinforced the dig's earthen walls. Other years had brought different manifestations of the curse, ranging from inconveniences to physical horrors, none of which he wanted to repeat.

But a curse was a curse was a curse, and want or no, he and his brother and sisters were stuck with it unless someone could figure out how to lift it.

From the time he was a child, Reg had been the one to claim that challenge. And he'd tried so hard, finding clues in family papers and relics, but nothing that actually panned out to anything concrete.

Anne had helped at first. He'd been an assistant professor at the University of Texas when she was hired as a lecturer in the English department. They'd met on the West Mall one spring day when the seam had ripped on her bookbag. From the first moment he'd seen her, she'd done something to him. If they'd been living centuries prior, he would have said she'd bewitched him, because once he saw her, he couldn't even see other women. She was all he wanted—to be with her, to work with her, to touch her and have her.

And the most amazing part of his infatuation was that she'd wanted him, too. Their romance had been intense and combustible, their bodies firing even without touch. And when they made love, he was certain that one day they would start a conflagration sufficient to rival the Chicago fire.

He closed his eyes and clenched his fists. *He would not miss her.*

But he did. Oh, how he did.

He finished off the second Scotch and almost called for another before stopping his finger as it hovered over the call button. *No.* He was about to step into April 1. He needed to keep his wits about him.

That, of course, had been another thing that he had loved about Anne: her utter acceptance when he'd told her about the curse. She hadn't told him he was imagining things, hadn't suggested that he speak to a counselor. She'd simply kissed him and told him that she'd help him break it.

"My family's from New Orleans, too," she'd said, when he told her that he believed the historic city was the source of the curse. "Most of them moved away long ago, but I've heard enough stories to believe in voodoo and magic and hexes and curses." She'd taken his hand on a Friday night. "Let's go this weekend and see what we can dig up about yours."

They hadn't been able to dig up much, just vague references to an "angel's amulet" that one of his eighteenth-century ancestors referred to circumspectly in a journal. From what they could gather, the amulet had been stolen by Timothy Franklin (the most ignoble of the then-ignoble Franklins), and although the value of the thing should have brought the family wealth, instead they suddenly found themselves wallowing in trouble, "which is as the witch had said," Olivia d'Espry, Timothy's wife had written in her journal. Olivia and Timothy Franklin were the only Franklins to have children, and Reg could trace his lineage back to them. He was grateful that Olivia preferred to write in her journal rather than do needlework as so many women of that time had done.

But even Olivia's journal revealed little. A few weeks after acquisition of the amulet, she'd written that one of Timothy's brothers had sought to dispose of the thing, but soon learned that it had gone missing.

He had hoped that the amulet's departure would be the end of their bad luck.

It wasn't.

Anne and Reg had spent the little spare time they could carve out of their teaching schedules to come to New Orleans and plow through whatever records they could locate. But try as they might, they found nothing. Nothing that could lead them to the missing amulet, or even describe it. All they knew was that it had the image of an angel carved upon it—Olivia Franklin had written that it was ironic that an angel could cause such harm.

They hadn't found the source of the curse or a solution, despite years of looking. The wasted time dragged Reg down, but Anne had squeezed his hand and reminded him that, at least, they'd found each other. And they had. They'd fallen in love.

And that simple fact about broke Reg's heart.

"That's silly," Anne had said, when he'd told her that they couldn't get married, that even their relationship put her at risk.

"Anne," he'd said. "I'm standing in a hospital. You've got a broken arm, a broken leg and a nasty gash in your hip." All of which she'd sustained trying to keep him from sliding down into a quarry when the ground beneath them had suddenly given way. On April 1, of course.

"You think that would make me not want you?" she'd argued. "Do my broken bones mean that you don't want me?"

"You know I do," he'd said. "Desperately. But I'm not going to stand by and watch you get hurt because of me."

Tears had streamed down her face. "If you leave me, I will be hurt because of you."

"But you'll be whole," he said.

She closed her eyes. "No. I won't."

Her words had almost weakened his resolve, but he knew he was right. *Knew it.* A cursed life was no life. Until he was able to remove the curse, he wasn't going to get married. Before Anne, marriage had been an abstract principle that didn't much bother him. Once he fell in love, though, his principles hurt him as much as the curse did.

She'd fought him on it, pointing out that most Franklins survived the curse, though she had to concede when he reminded her that some had died and many had been injured. And the injuries sometimes slid over onto spouses, too. Marriage, after all, would make her a Franklin.

"Isn't it enough that I don't care?" she'd asked. "That I'm willing to take that risk?"

He'd squeezed her hand, wanting so badly to pull her toward him and kiss her, to bury himself inside her and let passion fight the curse. Instead, he'd spoken calmly and evenly. "It's not a risk I'm willing to take."

After that, she hadn't tried to persuade him anymore. Instead, she'd quietly applied for other jobs, and ended up moving from Texas to New Orleans. They'd fought about it, of course, so loud the neighbors had complained, but in the end, they were both stubborn, and she left, her last words—that she loved him—hanging in the air.

Those words had cut him like a knife, and for the first time he could remember since childhood, Reg Franklin had cried.

He heard she'd moved into an old family property in the Garden District and now worked as a professor at Tulane. He'd fought the urge to get in his car and race to New Orleans. He needed to stay away, he knew. He'd made the right decision—that she was better without him—and he was afraid that if he saw her again, his resolve would fail.

Now he was going back to New Orleans, and he wasn't certain if he wanted to see her, or wanted her to stay far, far away.

Once again he looked at his watch. One minute past twelve. His stomach clenched, fearing a crash, and his gaze went automatically toward the window and the lights below. In his mind, he could see Anne down there. She'd always said that she'd catch him if he fell.

He doubted that this was what she meant.

He squeezed his eyes shut and told himself to sleep. If he was going to be sucked into a disaster, the best thing to do was sleep during the worst of it.

But sleep wouldn't come. Anne was on his mind now, though in truth she'd never been far from his thoughts the last two years.

He'd left Texas soon after she did. For over a year, he'd pursued any lead he could find on the curse with an insane frenzy, desperate to find an answer and get her back.

Then he realized there was no answer to be had. He wanted her still, so desperately, but he couldn't bring himself to put her in harm's way. Even the fact that Cam and Devon were happily married by then couldn't sway him, because as much as he loved them, he thought they were putting Jenna and Chance in horrible danger.

Now, of course, he had to admit that Jenna and

Chance were fine. Even Darcy had been engaged now for almost a year, and Evan was as healthy as a horse.

Reg, however, kept waiting for the other shoe to drop. When it did, he didn't want it dropping on Anne.

He'd left, because he knew he'd never solve the curse, and being on the same continent with her was just too damn painful.

He'd stopped trying to track down the amulet, because every blocked path reminded him of her and of what they couldn't have together.

He'd gone to England to escape her, and now he was coming back against his better judgment because Jean Michel had sent him an e-mail. An e-mail he had never expected to get, but which had such a solid clue that he felt like he had to take the chance.

If this worked, he'd crawl to Anne and beg forgiveness. But until then, he couldn't see her.

Seeing her and not having her would hurt too damn much.

He realized with a start that the plane had started its descent. The other first-class passengers around him seemed fine with that. Reg, of course, was terrified, and he clung to the arms of the seat, feeling clammy and unsure, his heart pounding in his chest, not even breathing until, finally, the wheels touched down. The overhead compartment above him popped open, and his carry-on bag came flying out, slamming hard into the aisle and startling the woman sitting one row up. He heard the crash of glass and was certain his shaving mirror had splintered.

Seven more years of bad luck, however, was a small price to pay for surviving the landing. If that was the worst of it, this would be his best April first ever.

Of course that wasn't the worst of it.

The airport was essentially empty, and the airline rep lined them all up to hand out hotel vouchers and give them tickets for the first plane to New Orleans in the morning.

No way was he getting back in a plane on April first.

He headed to the car rental counter, found the girl about to shut the gate and spent thirty minutes convincing her to rent him the last car on their lot, which turned out to be little more than a small box on wheels.

The drive from Houston to New Orleans took less than six hours without traffic, and he wasn't crazy about making it in a sardine can. He had no choice, though, and so he set off down Interstate 10, the traffic in the middle of the night light and the road free and open...for the first five miles.

After that, the traffic settled in.

Apparently the states of both Louisiana and Texas believed that the middle of the night on April Fools' Day was the best time to undertake road construction.

It took him eight hours to get to the French Quarter, and when he finally pulled his car into the valet area at the Chateau Vieux Carre hotel he was hot (the air conditioner in the car went out near Baton Rouge), tired and definitely grumpy.

"Franklin?" the clerk at the desk said, tapping the keys on her computer. "I'm sorry, sir. I don't show a reservation."

He resisted the urge to bang his head on the polished granite counter. "How about we forget the reservation and set me up for a room now."

"Of course, sir. No problem." She tapped some more and then smiled at him. "All set."

"Great. The key?"

Her eyes blinked owlishly. "I'm sorry, sir. Check-in isn't until three, but I can get you early check-in at eleven."

He looked at his watch. That would give him just enough time to walk over to Royal and meet Jean Michel at his antique shop. "Perfect. Can I leave my luggage?"

"No problem at all." She rang for a bellman who came over with practiced efficiency, then tagged Reg's bag and spirited it away.

He would have liked the chance to change clothes and splash some water on his face, and he considered waiting the forty-five minutes in the lobby. But he was also anxious to talk to Jean Michel. The antiques dealer had said he'd found something that Reg would want to see—something he didn't want to discuss in an e-mail—but something that Reg had been looking for.

Considering Reg and Anne had gone to Jean Michel back when they were trying to track down the amulet, Reg was hoping that was what his friend had found.

If so, he didn't want to wait a moment longer than necessary.

He rubbed his hands over his face to wake himself up, though the adrenalin of the search was easing the exhaustion from the long flight and drive.

Then he stepped through the front door onto Bourbon street, already bustling with tourists. He turned right, walked one block, then turned right again and continued on to Royal. He followed the street toward Canal, the route as familiar to him as breathing. When he was a block away, he saw the sign announcing "Michel Brothers, Antique and Estate Sales." He smiled, looking forward to seeing the wiry old man.

As he pushed through the doorway, however, his smile faded and his heart stuttered in his chest.

Jean was already at the counter, talking with another customer. They both turned as he entered, and Reg found himself staring into the fathomless brown eyes of the only woman he'd ever loved.

"Hello, Reg," Anne said. "I think you're going to want to see this."

2

ANNE DAWES CLUTCHED the display counter so hard she was certain the glass would shatter. But she kept her chin high, and she told herself she was doing fine. There was no way he could have seen how much his presence rattled her; no way he could know how startled she was to see him again, much less how much the bottom had fallen away from her stomach when she'd turned and seen the hard lines of his face and the piercing green of his eyes.

A green that had deepened like a forest when they'd made love and twinkled like carnival fire when he'd teased her.

She forced her smile wide, reminding herself that she'd moved on. He'd made it perfectly clear that he no longer cared about her, and Anne wasn't the kind of woman who hung around and pined for what she couldn't have, no matter how much she might want it. "Come see what Jean has discovered," she said. "I don't know if you care anymore, but—"

"I care," he said, his voice so low she almost couldn't hear him, and she mentally cursed herself, because she had *not* intended to go there. But it wasn't until that very moment that she realized how much it hurt that he'd blown off the search to undo the curse.

All this time, in fact, she'd assumed that he was still looking. That perhaps, one day he'd come back to her. Then two days ago she'd learned the truth when Jean Michel had come to her office to tell her about an interesting necklace at an estate sale. Interesting because of the angel carved into the charm, which consisted of some type of large amulet, as well as the intriguing inscription inside the piece if one pried it open at a hidden hinge-point. "I wasn't sure if Reginald would come," he said. "He says he's no longer searching, but I thought something like this…"

He'd trailed off, clearly assuming that she already knew that Reg had given up. "Yes," she'd said, forcing her voice not to shake. "For something like this, he'd probably come."

Not that she fully understood what *this* was. Jean Michel had refused to tell her what the inscription said, requiring her to visit his shop this morning if she was inclined to find out.

She almost didn't come. After all, what did she care anymore?

She'd put her pride and her heart on the line when she told Reg she'd cared only for him and not the damn curse. That she wanted him more than she'd ever wanted anyone, or could ever imagine wanting anyone in the future. She'd practically begged him to marry her, and now she was humiliated by the way she'd revealed so much to him.

If only he'd pulled her to him… But instead he'd pushed her away, and the hot blush of shame now covered not only her cheeks, but her whole life. He'd always insisted that he wanted her desperately, but not with the curse. She'd just as stubbornly insisted that she didn't care.

But he'd made it clear that he did care, and when it was obvious that their relationship wouldn't progress because of his damn obsession with that damn curse, she'd moved to Louisiana.

Soon after, she'd heard through the grapevine that he'd moved to England. And then she'd learned, through Jean Michel, that he wasn't pursuing the curse anymore.

The knowledge had stung. Because if he wasn't looking to end the curse, that also meant that he wasn't looking to ever get back together with her.

A selfish reaction, maybe, since she'd been the first one to walk away, but that didn't change the fact that her heart hurt. And now that he was standing in front of her, she truly realized the depth of that ache.

He crossed the dark, almost musty antique shop in five long strides, then paused beside her, not touching her but gazing at her with an intensity so strong it almost felt a caress. "Hello, Anne," he said. "It's good to see you again."

She looked away, managing only a nod because her voice didn't seem to be working anymore. She didn't want to want him, but she did. Damn him all to hell, one look at him—one glimpse—and she wanted nothing more than to touch him.

It was an impulse she intended to fight, because she knew damn well it would lead nowhere good.

"Jean," he said, shaking hands with the elderly shop-keeper. "What have you found?"

The wiry old man smiled, so obviously excited about his discovery that his words began to wear away at Anne's sharp edges. "Complete bonne chance," he said in the false French accent he maintained for benefit of the tourists. "I was at an estate sale, you see, going through the belongings of a family that had sold their home in the Garden District after Katrina. They'd tried for years to restore the house, but simply couldn't manage it." He shook his head, making a sympathetic noise. "Sad, very sad," he added, the accent now gone. "In a box of jewelry, I found this." He reached under the cabinet and drew out the necklace. He'd described it to Anne earlier, but the description didn't do it justice.

The amulet was large, the size of a baby's fist, and teardrop shaped. A purple stone filled the center of one side, and on the back, etched into the gold, was the delicate image of an angel.

"Olivia's journal," Reg said, his voice little more than a whisper. "Do you think…?"

"I do," Jean Michel said. "I wouldn't have called you otherwise."

She saw the glint of hope in Reg's eyes, followed by wariness. "There must be many amulets with angels. For that matter, we don't even know that the amulet had an angel carved on it. Perhaps it simply belonged to a pretty girl."

"Possible," Jean said. "Which is why your quest has been so unfruitful, correct?"

Reg had to concede he was right, and as he did, he looked sideways at Anne with such a look of loss and regret that she had to reach out and grab the counter once again. She'd been certain that his heart had abandoned her. Seeing the heat in his eyes now, she had to rethink that notion.

No, she corrected. Not heat. Something more. Desire,

yes. But not merely sexual. What she saw when he looked at her was herself reflected back, as if he wanted *her*—all of her—and not just her body.

Dammit, she was going to have to strangle Jean. There'd been no need to pull her into this.

To make her once again want what she knew she couldn't have.

"Don't you think?"

She blinked, then realized that they'd been talking to her. "What?"

Jean Michel smiled. "I said we should open the amulet and see if we can't convince Mr. Franklin that this piece is in fact relevant to his search, don't you think?"

"I don't know," she said. "You haven't told me what you found inside."

"True," he said, the lines around his eyes crinkling. "I told you only that I was certain. And now I will prove it to the two of you at the same time." He held the amulet out to her. "The item belonged to a woman. It is only fitting that a woman should open it."

He placed the amulet in her hand, the chain twisting into her palm. It was lighter than she would have expected, and she realized that it was hollow. Carefully, she examined the piece, then found the small gap between the halves. She slid her thumbnail in and felt a pop as the clasp gave. The amulet opened like a clamshell, revealing a hollow interior, much like that of a locket, only with a greater volume. She'd read about such items, and knew that often they concealed contraband such as opiates or poisons. This amulet concealed nothing but a message, the text in French but easily translatable.

Steal our honor
Steal our soul
Thou shalt pay with the gravest of fortune
Until the soul of us is returned
To swell the heart of an angel
Who sings glory on high

She looked from Jean to Reg. "What does it mean?"

"I don't know yet," Reg said. "But I think Jean is right. This is the amulet Olivia mentions." He pointed to the opposing side from the inscription, and when Anne leaned in close, she saw the initials *TF* scraped into the gold, as if with the end of a knife. "Timothy Franklin, possibly? Olivia's husband." He met her eyes, and she saw the hint of excitement, so familiar from when they'd been on the chase together. "If I'm right— and if I can truly resolve the history of this piece—then maybe I can finally bring an end to this curse."

He met her eyes, and she held her breath, waiting for the words that didn't come. Words that would say *why*, other than his family and his safety and his own well-being, he would want the curse lifted. Wanting to hear him say he wanted her.

He didn't say it, and she felt like a fool, all the more so because after three years, she really should be over him. It really shouldn't hurt anymore.

"Who did you acquire this from?" Reg asked, his attention on Jean.

"A young woman named Libby." The dealer was already writing the woman's information on the back of a business card. "I don't think she knows much, but perhaps enough to get you started."

Reg pocketed the card, then held out his hand for the amulet. Anne pressed it into his palm, her skin sharp with awareness when she brushed his hand. If the room had been dark, she believed that sparks would have popped with the contact, but Reg's face stayed flat, his eyes on Jean and not on her, and Anne couldn't tell if he didn't feel it, or if he felt too much.

She hoped for the latter, and at the same time hated herself for even letting the thought into her head.

She shouldn't have come. This wasn't her quest anymore. She needed to leave.

"How much do I owe you?" Reg asked, pulling out his wallet.

Jean Michel shook his head. "For today, consider it a loaner. If it turns out to truly be the amulet you seek, you can come back and I will charge you through the nose."

Reg laughed and the men shook hands.

She stood watching them, wanting to simply walk away. After all, this wasn't her problem anymore. Reg was here, and he hadn't even called her to tell her he was coming. He didn't need her any more and staying bordered on pathetic.

She didn't consider herself pathetic. Or needy. Or clingy.

Where Reg was concerned, though, she constantly feared that she could fall into those horrible tendencies simply because he overloaded her. Her senses, her desire.

Her wants.

Go. Go now, before it's too hard to walk away.

"I'm staying at the Vieux Carre," he said, his voice almost casual, but with enough edge to it that she understood the cost of the words.

"My car is parked near there," she said, meeting his eyes and lifting her chin, as if to prove to him that she was still whole despite the way he'd been ripped from her. "I'll walk there with you."

They said goodbye to Jean and walked down Royal in silence, not speaking until they'd turned the corner.

"You moved to England," she said, unable to keep the accusation out of her voice. But it wasn't the move that bothered her; it was what it represented.

"You moved to New Orleans."

She closed her eyes against the harshness of his words, the tightness of his body, and, mostly, against the heat she saw reflected in his face, a desire that was so familiar, a desire she had assumed she would never see again.

"I had to," she said, her voice breaking. "We've had this conversation before. You wouldn't…and I couldn't stay, not if staying meant waiting forever." What she couldn't say out loud, though, was that the distance hadn't mattered. No matter what her motives, she hadn't stopped waiting. Not really.

He reached out his hand for her, then pulled it back quickly as if the gesture had been unintentional and foolish. "I couldn't risk you. Not you."

She stopped walking, the emotion in his voice making her feel both cherished and angry. Cherished, because she truly believed that he cared. Angry, because he obviously hadn't cared enough to keep looking.

And angrier still because he'd taken the choice entirely upon himself, never letting her have a say.

"Anne?"

"You stopped looking," she said, her words an accusation, a weapon.

The weapon hit home; she saw him flinch.

"I couldn't stand it anymore," he said, and there was real pain in his voice. "Not knowing where to go next. Thinking I'd found a lead only to have it dry up in my fingers. I'd gone down every avenue, searched every place, and I knew it would never be over. And yet each time I found a possibility, I thought of you. And I hoped." He closed his eyes, his throat moving as he swallowed. "After a while, I couldn't take it anymore, and I knew I had to stop. Just stop."

"Without me," she said, then mentally kicked herself for sounding so openly, desperately needy.

"What I believe hadn't changed," he said. "Marrying into a curse…" He trailed off with a shake of his head.

"*Had*n't changed?" she asked, because she was an English professor, and a subtle change in tense or word choice could somehow make all the difference.

He didn't comment, but started walking again. Despite herself, hope flared within Anne. She hurried to keep up.

"I hear Cam and Jenna are doing well," she said casually, as they turned onto Bourbon street.

"They're very happy," he said, after a short pause. She wondered what the admission cost him.

"And Devon and Chance," she continued. "I haven't talked to them myself, but Darcy says they're doing fine. She was at Tulane for a seminar a few months ago. Apparently she's doing great, too. What's his name? Ethan?"

"Evan," Reg corrected. "And they're all doing great."

"Hmmm."

"They're not you," he said. "And I saw the woman I love broken and battered, and dammit, I couldn't stand it."

"I'm not battered anymore," she whispered, hanging on to another key word: *love*. And in the present tense.

She barely dared to hope.

They'd reached the entrance to his hotel, and he slid past the doorman, not answering, and headed straight for the front desk. "Reg Franklin," he said. "I'm here to check in."

Anne leaned on the counter beside him, knowing it was time to say goodbye. This was his fight, and if he didn't want her—or if he wasn't willing to admit he wanted her—then she needed to leave. This man had already broken her heart once. She really didn't want to stand by while he did it again.

For some reason, though, she didn't leave.

"Franklin?" the clerk was saying as she tapped on her computer. "I'm so sorry, Mr. Franklin, but we don't seem to have a reservation for you."

3

REG STARED AT THE WOMAN behind the counter. "Could you repeat that?"

"I said we don't have a reservation for Franklin. I'm sorry. Could I get your confirmation number?"

He clenched his fists at his sides, mentally kicking himself for not having the earlier girl write it down or print him a receipt. "I don't have one."

She looked at him as if he were something she'd scraped off her shoe. "I see. One moment."

She started to type, and he leaned against the counter, as if proximity would result in a room. Beside him, Anne stood frowning.

"I was here earlier. I talked to a woman standing right where you are now. She said my room would be ready at eleven. Your people checked my bag."

The girl's brow lifted, as if that somehow made him legitimate. "Can I see the bellman's receipt?"

"Of course," he said, relieved that this was going to get all worked out. He fumbled in his pocket, came up with a few scraps of paper, a dollar coin and a paperclip, but didn't find the bell ticket. "Damn."

The clerk's eyes rose. "Are you sure you're in the right hotel?"

He bit back a particularly nasty curse, then calmed when Anne's hand pressed softly on his forearm. "You know what this is," she said. "Why don't you stay the night at my house? By tomorrow, I bet your hotel situation will be all worked out."

"I don't know," he said. Already her nearness was messing with his head, not to mention his body. He'd never wanted to cut her out of his life. Hell, for many of the past years, he'd been trying to end this curse, not for the family good, but for her. Because he wanted her so desperately.

So desperately, in fact, that he'd gone all the way to England to escape the desire.

And yet here she was and here he was, and if anyone should realize it, a Franklin should know that you can never escape Fate. If something is meant to be, then it simply is.

Once upon a time, he'd thought that he and Anne were meant to be, and seeing her now, he still thought so.

What he didn't know how to do was reconcile his need to keep her safe with his need to touch her, to make love to her, to have her once again in his arms and in his bed.

Dammit all, he was a wreck.

"Reg." She was tugging on his arm, her fingers slipping down and twining with his as she pulled him away from the counter, the clerk eyeing them both suspiciously. Reg barely noticed the clerk's confused looks, though. All he could think about—all he could feel— was Anne's fingers pressed soft against his.

"*Anne.*" Her name came out raw and desperate, which was exactly how he felt, but he wished it weren't so obvious. "I don't think that's a good idea."

"Why not?" Her eyes were wide and guileless. "You need a place, and my house is huge. And unlike a hotel, if you break something expensive, I'll understand it's because of the curse. I doubt the manager here would be so accommodating."

Her words made him grin, her easy acceptance of this curse that he had to bear making him feel normal. More than that, making him feel like he could beat it.

He knew better, though. This was April first, and that meant if she was with him, she wasn't safe, either.

He should leave her now and follow this lead by himself. He should stand right there and very firmly state that this was his problem, and his alone.

But he didn't have the strength. Now that he saw her again—now that he'd touched her again—he couldn't walk away.

Selfish, but he had to have at least a few more moments with her.

A few more moments, and, maybe, if they broke this curse, if she still wanted it, just maybe those moments could grow into a lifetime.

And if they didn't break it?

Well, then at least he would have those precious minutes to add to his memories of Anne.

"Reg," she said, her voice taking on a firm, no-nonsense tone. "You need to come with me. You're exhausted. When was the last time you slept?"

"I can't sleep," he countered. "I need answers."

"You do. But you're not going to find them in a hotel." Her fingers tightened on his. "Please. Let me take you home."

Hope flowed over him, because this was what he

wanted, and what he couldn't have unless the curse was abated. He wanted to push back the hope, and Anne along with it. Because hadn't he thought he could beat it before? And hadn't he failed?

Today, though…

Today, for the first time, he had a lead that felt right. *The amulet.*

And if it really was the solution…if Anne really did still want him…

"Reg?" she pressed.

Maybe it was a mistake. He didn't know. All he knew was that he couldn't stand walking away from her again now that she was beside him. Whatever else he did today, he was going to end this damn curse.

He was going to end it, and he was going to win back the woman he had never stopped loving.

PROFESSOR REGINALD Franklin, the esteemed archeologist currently drawing a paycheck from the illustrious Oxford University in jolly old England, sucked on his knuckle while he slept.

It wasn't as cute as if he actually sucked his thumb, but Anne thought the habit was absolutely charming. She'd forgotten about it, but seeing him now, leaning against the window of her Camry, his knuckle pressed against his mouth, her heart did a little flip-flop as she thought about all those nights she hadn't seen him. Enough nights lost to give her sufficient time to forget.

She hadn't wanted to forget, and once upon a time, she hadn't believed forgetting was possible. She loved this man; how could any detail of him ever escape her memory?

It wouldn't again, she vowed. This time, she was keeping him.

If she had to prowl the seedy sections of the city and find herself a voodoo priestess to simply overpower the old curse, then she would. Or put a curse on her. He could hardly tell her she was safer without him if she was cursed on April first, too.

Something, *anything,* to keep him with her. Because now that he was there beside her again, there was no way she was letting him go.

The drive to her house was short—the Garden District was only a few miles from the French Quarter—but she took the long way simply so that he could get a few more minutes of sleep. She considered driving for hours, but she knew he wouldn't appreciate it. He had a lead, and he wanted to follow it.

She approached her house from the side street, then pulled around, up her driveway, and came to a halt under the *porte cochiere.* He woke up the moment she killed the engine, just as she'd expected he would. Just as she always remembered he had.

"Come on," she said. "I'd tell you to grab your luggage, but…"

He narrowed his eyes. "Thanks for reminding me."

The house had been restored in stunning detail by a distant cousin who'd accepted a job offer in California. Fortunately, the building hadn't suffered any serious damage during Hurricane Katrina. Unfortunately, the cousin had never gotten around to buying period furniture. So Anne had moved into a fabulously restored house with Wal-Mart furniture.

"It's beautiful," Reg said, glancing around the

parlor. She tried to see it through his eyes—the hard wood, the mullioned windows, the crystal chandelier. If the card table by the door bothered him, he didn't let on.

"It is," she agreed. "And it'll get even better. My hobby lately is to look for period pieces. That's one of the reasons Jean Michel and I have kept in touch."

He looked at her. "One of the reasons?"

Heat flooded her cheeks, and she told herself she had no reason to be embarrassed. The way she felt about Reg wasn't a secret. It was a hard reality that they'd both had trouble living with. "We also talk about you," she said. "He called me because of the amulet. Because he knows that I want to find an end to the curse."

"Want?" he repeated, taking a step toward her, the air between them seeming to crackle as he moved. "Not *wanted?*" His lips curved, and she saw both victory and sadness in his eyes. "As an English professor, you should know the value of accuracy. Of making sure you're speaking in the correct tense."

"I do," she said, her words coming out in a breathless whisper.

Another step toward her. She held her ground, forcing herself not to retreat. "And you still want to solve the curse? After everything I've put you through?"

Maybe she shouldn't. Maybe she was a fool for wanting him so badly even now that he'd made it clear that there was only one set of conditions by which he would have her. But she couldn't help it. She did. She had. And she always would.

She didn't need to speak; she could tell that he saw her answer in her eyes.

Slowly, he reached out and brushed her cheek, and it was only when he did that she realized that she was crying. "I'm sorry," she said. "I'm a mess."

"Only because I made you one," he said, taking a step toward her. "I'd understand if you hate me."

"Sometimes I want to," she admitted. "But no. I don't hate you." *Far from it.*

"Anne." His voice was thick with need, and she didn't protest when he slid his hand along the back of her neck, or when he leaned in close. Not even when his lips touched hers.

He tasted like her memories, decadent and sweet, erotic and safe.

Safe. Wasn't that ironic? A man living under a curse—a man who'd broken her heart—and yet it was in his arms that she felt the safest she'd ever felt.

At the moment though, she didn't care about irony or curses. She cared only for his lips, firm and demanding, upon her own. His tongue, sweeping inside her mouth, pulling her in, as if he wanted to consume her, to do battle with her, and leave them both gasping for breath in the heat of the aftermath.

She curled her arms around him, pulling him closer, needing him closer. More than that, simply *needing* him. She felt his muscles beneath his shirt, taut and ready, like a man holding back. And although she wanted him to let go, she also knew what he was fighting—desire versus duty.

And if she knew Reg, duty would win.

Regretfully, she pulled back, breaking the kiss. "Later," she said. "After we call Libby."

He eyed her thoughtfully, then nodded and pulled out

his cell phone. "Battery's dead," he said, then rolled his eyes. "April first."

She passed him her phone, and he dialed the number, then sat silently for a moment, his eyes on her and the phone pressed to his ear. After a moment, he left a name and number on Libby's answering machine and asked her to call back at her earliest convenience. Then he passed the phone back to Anne, their fingers brushing with the transfer, and the contact sending an electric current dancing up her arm.

"Now we wait," he said, moving closer. "And I think I know the perfect way to pass the time."

4

REG HELD HIS BREATH, knowing that he was being bold, acting only on his own desires and what he hoped— *prayed*—that he saw in Anne's eyes.

She had every right to shoot him down, every right to tell him to take a fast train to a hot hell, but he really hoped she wouldn't.

And then, as if he were a better man than he was— a man who deserved good things, a man who wasn't cursed this particular day—she stepped closer to him, her expression glowing and her eyes defiant, yet at the same time soft with expectation. "What?" she whispered. "What can we do to pass the time?"

There was no invitation in her words. But in her tone...

Oh, dear Lord, her tone held both an invitation and a demand, and Reg accepted both gratefully. Helplessly. With a desperation borne of three long years apart.

"Anne," he whispered, his voice raw as he took her hand and pulled her close. "Dear God, Anne."

She didn't answer, instead tilting her head up to look at him as a wisp of a smile touched her lips. "No curse," she whispered. "The opposite, I think. You're here, aren't you?"

His heart twisted with the words, and with the knowledge of all the time they'd been apart because of the curse. Right then, though, she was right. At that moment, they were together, and there was no bad luck pushing them apart. It was just Anne and Reg and a passion between them he'd known he would never forget, but hadn't believed he would ever experience again.

"Thank God I came," he said.

She laughed, apparently delighted by the desperation in his voice. "We'll send Jean Michel a thank-you gift."

"Hell, yes. We'll buy him a small country."

"Reg?"

"Yeah?"

"Shut up and kiss me."

That was one idea with which he wasn't about to argue, and he pulled her close, his palm cupping her face as his lips closed over hers. She tasted as he remembered, as he'd known she would, like mint and coffee, and the memory fired his senses as much as her touch did. His body was tight with need, desperate to rekindle what they'd had and, more than that, to make it grow. To make it fresh and new.

"You're beautiful," he said, meaning every word. Her dark hair and dark eyes fit the house like an exotic ornament. Her skin, so light it was almost translucent, gave her an ethereal quality and hid a bone-deep strength of conviction that he admired—and that had often flummoxed him.

"God, Reg, I've missed you. I...I want—"

"So do I," he said, then saw the devious curve of her lips, as her hand slid down his back, then around his hips to cup his firm erection.

"Yeah," she whispered. "I guess you do."

"Anne." He hoped to never stop saying her name.

"My bedroom's upstairs."

"Too damn far."

"There's a couch in the parlor."

Laughing like teenagers, they moved hand in hand to the parlor. She sat on a plush red velvet couch, then patted the space beside her for him. He didn't take the offer. Instead, he knelt in front of her, his hands on her thighs. He eased her legs apart, then inched closer until his body pressed against the edge of the chaise, and his hands stroked upward, finding her shirt. He tugged it free, then let his hands graze upward, watching in rapt fascination the way her muscles twitched and her skin tightened, listening in awed rapture to the small, soft noises she made as his fingertips brushed her bare skin. "Reg…"

"Hush," he said, then went to work on the buttons of her shirt. They were small, and his fingers felt large and clumsy, but he got them open, then pulled the halves of her shirt apart. Her nipples were hard beneath the lace of her white bra, the aureolas brown and puckered, as if waiting for him to kiss them.

He wasn't about to hesitate, and he tugged the lace down, drawing her breast free, then closed his mouth over it, electricity shooting through him from the contact, and his cock hardening from the sound of her gentle cry of "oh" coupled with her hands clutching hard to his shoulders. *That was Anne*, he thought. *Softness and steel.*

And then he stopped thinking altogether, concentrating only on the pleasure of her body.

His mouth moved from her breast up her delicate collarbone, then to her ear, his tongue sweeping in, knowing what made her wet, wanting her as turned on as he was.

Her moan told him that his memories hadn't lied. Her fingers in his hair moved with desperate urgency. "Reg, please," she whispered, and he stroked his hands down, down, cupping her sex through her jeans, then feeling a wash of male satisfaction as she writhed against him. "Dear Lord," she said, her own hands moving, grasping, touching, and his cock hardening in response, although he didn't see how he could get any harder than he already was.

Her lips were on his neck suddenly, and she was leaning forward, no longer content to sit back as he made love to her. Her fingers eased down, finding the button of his fly even as his own fingers were pulling down her zipper. He let one finger slip inside, easing between denim and satin, then groaned when he found her panties soaked. The groan transformed into one of pure pleasure when her soft fingers cupped his cock through the khaki of his own pants.

"Off," he said, and she nodded mutely, then started fumbling at her clothes. He did the same, saying a silent thank-you to whoever invented slip-on shoes, then immediately forgetting his damn shoes when he saw Anne, stretched out on the chaise, wearing a sultry smile on her face, and not a single stitch of clothing.

"It's April Fools' Day," he said as the sun streaming in from around the edges of the closed curtains cut shafts of light over her body. "I'm afraid if I blink you'll disappear."

"I'm not going anywhere again," she said, her eyes meeting his. "Are you?"

He didn't answer—he couldn't. Nothing had changed, not really. And yet this felt right, and the three years they'd been apart felt so very wrong.

She must have seen the conflict on his face, because

she shook her head, and flashed a sad, quick smile. "I don't need an answer right now," she said. "Right now, I only need you."

Thank God for that.

He moved to straddle her, his skin so sensitive that the slightest brush of breath against it could send him over the edge. He craved her like he'd never craved anything before, and he wanted nothing more than to please her, to live up to the desire he saw in her eyes. And the love.

He touched her gently at first, but he couldn't remain gentle, and when she urged him on, he spread her legs and found the core of her. He slid his hands over her, feeling her slick wet heat, knowing that he wouldn't last long. He'd put a condom in his wallet—at the time, he hadn't known why, since he hadn't slept with a woman since Anne had left. Now, of course, he knew. It was because of her, and when he sheathed himself and slid inside, he seemed to fit her perfectly, her body closing around him like a glove, the small contractions of her muscles drawing him in, growing stronger as her breath grew more strangled and as reality seemed to spin away leaving nothing but the moment. Nothing but them, together, floating high, coming nearer and nearer to some unknown destination until, finally, he realized it wasn't the destination that mattered but merely that they were coming.

Coming.

And that was when he shattered, the world, the universe, his body exploding, and Anne's too, as she clung to him, fingernails digging into his back, her legs hooked around his waist pulling him closer and tighter, as if trying to milk every last instant from the moment, every last tremor and pulse of pleasure.

"Wow," he said, his arms no longer capable of holding him up. He rolled to the side, his back against the couch, his arms cradling her. They were both coated in a fine sheen of sweat, and for a few minutes, or possibly an eternity, they simply lay there. Then she rolled over, pressing her face against his chest so that her breath cooled his damp body. "What happens if we don't solve the curse?" she asked, not looking up. "Are you just going to walk out on me again?"

He looked down at the dark curls of her head, but he couldn't see her face. He couldn't answer. He didn't know what the answer was.

She tilted her head up, and he realized she'd taken hope from his hesitation. "It's getting less, you know," she said. "Years ago, the stories tell of Franklins dying. Now, you lose out on a hotel reservation."

He looked away, wishing he could be certain she was right, but unable to get the picture of her in the hospital out of his mind.

"Reg?"

He closed his eyes and sighed. He'd sold his house when he'd moved to England. There, he was renting a room from another professor. He was, by all standards, drifting.

Or he had been a few hours before.

Now, he knew, he'd come home. Anne was home.

Trouble was, he still wasn't sure that home was a safe place to be.

HER BREATH SKIPPED IN HER throat, and she wished she could take back her words, and only keep the touches. It was the touches between them that were real. The words, though… She was afraid that with words, he could talk himself into leaving again. That was something she so very much did not want to happen.

She'd been going through the motions, living here without him. She hadn't even realized it until he'd walked back into her life, but now she saw it. They were like two halves of a whole, and now that he was back, she couldn't let him go again.

But she didn't know how to make him stay.

"Kiss me again," she said, because she was scared to let go of him, and because this was what they were made to do, to be: one. "Please," she said, stroking his hair out of his face and looking into his eyes. "Make love to me again."

They went slow this time, so slow that it seemed that every inch of her body fired beneath his touch. And when he slid into her, it was as if he was an extension of her body. They moved together, one mind and one heart, and she wished she could draw him inside her body and keep him safe from the curse, safe with her forever.

Her orgasm came this time not as an explosion, but as a rising crescendo. As the world floated away on color and music, the last three years evaporated.

This was the life she wanted—*the man she wanted*—and no matter what, she was going to keep him.

The question of *how* was still preying on her mind when her phone rang. He lifted his head from where it rested on her breast and met her eyes. "Libby?" she asked.

"Probably."

She felt her pulse rate increase with excitement. If this worked…if they really could vanquish the curse…

He shifted over her to grab her phone, then glanced

at the caller ID. "It's her," he said, then answered the phone. But he kept his hand on her thigh, as if silently saying that under normal circumstances he would ignore the phone in favor of touching her. These, however, weren't normal circumstances, and she fully supported anything that might lead them to the end of this curse.

She listened as Reg explained about finding the amulet and about how he was trying to trace back its ownership. He searched for a pen, then scribbled an address. Finally, he ended the call and smiled up at her. "She's on her lunch break until one-thirty, and she's willing to meet with us." He stood and held out his arm. "Feel like a burger from Camillia Grill?"

The quaint restaurant at the end of St. Charles was, in fact, one of Anne's favorite places. They drove instead of taking the trolley simply to ensure they had enough time to speak with Libby. A good choice, it turned out, because Libby was a talker. And not necessarily about the amulet. No, Libby liked to talk about everything.

"I used to not eat meat," she said, shoving a mass of mauve ringlets back from her face. "But then I went to this cook-out in my friend's backyard, and oh my gosh, it just smelled so good, and from that day on, I was a certified burger addict all over again." She took a big bite out of her cheeseburger. "Damn, but this is my idea of heaven."

Anne and Reg were sitting on either side of her at the counter, and they exchanged amused looks before Reg pushed his plate of fries toward her. "I've always thought a burger was only as good as the fries that came with it. Want one?"

She took two and shoved them into her mouth. While she chewed, he pulled out the amulet.

"Oh! Look! It's all shined up. A pretty trinket."

"Trinket?"

She shrugged. "I know it's gold—and that Jean Michel gave me a good price. But it's kind of gaudy, you know?"

"It is a bit," Anne said. "But it's not the design we're interested in. It's the history."

Libby rolled her eyes. "Don't know how much help I'm gonna be. It's not even from my family, you know?"

Anne glanced to Reg, alarmed. "What do you mean?" he asked.

"It was my stepmother's," she said, then took another huge bite of burger. "Oh, man," she said, her mouth full. "Ambrosia. I swear, this is ambrosia."

"What do you know about your stepmother?" Reg asked, pushing the plate even closer to her.

"Not a whole lot. She's a pain in the butt, really, but I guess when you consider her family, that's no big shock."

"Her family?"

Libby shrugged. "Oh, it's not like they're famous or anything. Well, except one."

"And the one?"

She rolls her eyes. "Mirabelle Rousseau. She lived back in the eighteenth century or something."

"Why was she famous?"

"It's bullshit, of course," Libby said. "But the whole freaking family thought she was a witch."

5

REG WORKED HARD NOT TO LET his excitement show on his face, but he was pretty sure he failed. After all, he could see clearly enough his own feelings reflected in Anne's eyes.

A witch.

It was just as Olivia's journal had referenced, and the timing was right. The eighteenth century. Back when Timothy Franklin was getting into trouble with women of questionable character.

It wasn't a stretch to assume that Timothy had bedded Mirabelle, seen the amulet and taken it.

Mirabelle realized who took it, and let it be known that she would take her revenge—and she would take it through witchcraft if necessary.

Considering the curse he now lived under, he had a feeling Mirabelle's assumed threat wasn't idle.

What didn't make sense, though, was why the curse still existed if Mirabelle got her amulet back. Either they were chasing the wrong story, or Mirabelle held a grudge.

He was banking that it was the latter.

"Do you know anything else?" Anne asked the girl.

"What? About Mirabelle, you mean?"

"Anything at all might help."

"Well, gosh. I heard that she collected statues of angels."

Reg caught Anne's eye, remembering the reference to angels in the inscription. "Interesting."

Libby rolled her eyes. "Weird, actually. 'Cause while she's off collecting angels, she's also supposedly cursing people. Made them have bad luck." She wiggled her fingers. "Whoo woo, and all that."

"Whoo woo," Reg repeated, the irony heavy in his voice.

"It's stupid," Libby said, "but what the hell do I know? Maybe it would be cool."

"Cool?" Reg knew he shouldn't ask—that he should keep her on point—but he was too curious about what she meant.

"Sure. I mean, hell, there was no curse on my family, but they still got wiped out. First the damn hurricane, then my dad's stroke. And it was just bad luck. Woulda been nice to have a curse to blame it on. At least then stuff wouldn't be so random."

"Random," he repeated.

"You know. Like what they say. 'Life happens' and all that bullshit."

He looked at Anne, his chest suddenly tight. "Right. All that bullshit." A moment passed, and as it did, it seemed to Reg that something within him was shifting, even though he couldn't quite grasp what it was. Now, however, wasn't the time for introspection. He needed to learn what this woman knew.

"Anything else you can think of?" Anne asked, as if reading his mind.

Libby's forehead scrunched up. "Well, I know that some of her descendants donated a ton of money to build a church a couple of generations ago." She rolled her eyes. "I know because I got dragged to mass there, and I'm not even Catholic. I guess they figured a church makes up for having a witch in the family. And I know she lived more than ninety years, and was one of the first people buried in Lafayette Cemetery." She swiveled on her stool to look at them both. "Does that help you any?"

Fifteen minutes later, Anne and Reg were pondering that very question. "Does it?" Anne asked as they walked through Lafayette Cemetery Number One, just a few blocks up the road from Camillia Grill. What better place, after all, to find an angel?

They were holding hands, and if you ignored the fact that they were walking among the dead, the afternoon felt wonderful. Like he'd asked her for a date, and now they were taking a walk through the park. A normal, typical, pleasant afternoon. It was, he thought, just a little bit like heaven.

"If Franklin didn't actually return the amulet," Anne began.

"And if it was Mirabelle who took it back herself," he continued, picking up her thread.

"Then that probably wouldn't be a reason for her to remove the curse," she finished. "So that means a Franklin needs to return her amulet."

"That's the plan," he said.

"And when you do—when *we*—do, then the curse will be lifted." She smiled brightly. "Of course, maybe it's a moot point. Nothing bad's happened since you lost your hotel reservation."

"The other shoe's waiting to drop," he said, but he smiled as he spoke.

She shook her head in mock exasperation. Or real frustration, he amended, as soon as he heard the harsh tone of her voice. "Dammit, Reg. You've got to accept that even if you can't end it, you can live with it. *We* can live with it."

"We are going to end it," he said, because he was determined not to fail today. He'd come to end this curse, he was the closest he had ever been, and he was not about to back off now.

"Good," she said. "Great. I hope we do. But *if* we don't, take a look around. We've gone most of the day with very little bad luck. Your siblings are happy with their spouses, and they're entirely intact. Your plane didn't fall out of the sky. My house didn't collapse around our ears. The curse is weakening. With each generation, it's less of a threat. Dammit, Reg, don't you see? It's whittling away to nothing, and in the meantime, I love you."

Her words cut through him, sharp and terrifying even while they buoyed him up. All his fears, all his walking away, and still she loved him.

"This is it," Anne said, looking at a raised stone grave. "See?" She nodded to the plaque with Mirabelle's name engraved. She hadn't been put into a family tomb, as most of the people in the cemetery, and they couldn't find anyplace to leave the amulet.

"Maybe we open the grave?"

She frowned. "Ick, but maybe." She looked up at him and he couldn't help but smile at her. Yeah, maybe they needed to open the sarcophagus, but he had something to say first. "Anne," he said. "I love you, too."

He watched her smile bloom wide, and felt his heart lift.

"Then forget the damn curse," she said. She grabbed him by the belt loops and pulled him against the stone tombs next to Mirabelle's grave. He buried his fingers in her hair and pulled her mouth to his, wanting to tell her that nothing in the world would make him forget it. The question was, could he live with it.

He didn't get the chance to speak, though, because suddenly they were tumbling backwards, falling into the crumbling remains of the tomb against which they'd been leaning. "Shit!" He leaped to his feet, then started pulling rubble off of Anne. "Dammit, don't you dare be hurt. Anne! Anne!"

"I'm okay." Her voice was soft, but strong, and limb by limb, she wiggled her body. "Yeah. I'm okay."

He sat back on his heels, his heart pounding, and Libby's words running through his head. *Life happens*.

Yeah, he thought, it did.

And so did curses. Hell, he knew that better than anyone.

The question was, if he was going to be cursed, did he want to be doomed with or without the woman he loved?

The answer was the same as it always had been: he wanted to be with Anne.

But today…

Well, today, maybe he'd finally realized that Anne understood what being with him meant, and it was her decision, too.

He took a deep breath, savoring the moment, then held out his hand. "Come on, sweetheart," he said. "Let's go home."

"Home?" She blinked. "What about the curse? The sarcophagus?"

He glanced sideways at it. "I guess we'll learn to live with it."

She clutched his hand and climbed to her feet. "What? Reg?"

"You're right. Hell, Libby was right."

Her eyes widened, and she hooked her arms around his neck, then pressed a soft kiss to his lips. "Reg Franklin, I love you."

"I love you, too," he said, meaning it more than he could ever express.

"Do you mean it? About the curse not mattering to you anymore?"

"I mean it."

She nodded, her expression pensive.

"Anne? What is it?"

"I'm not sure now if I should even say, but I think I've figured it out." She brushed her palm against his cheek. "I know where to take the amulet."

THEY HAD TO CALL LIBBY to be sure, but then they headed straight from the cemetery to St. Theresa's Church on Poydras. The small church that had received funding from Mirabelle's family. Funding and statuary.

"The angels," Anne had said. "The inscription talked about returning it to the soul of the angel, right?"

"Right."

"Well, if Mirabelle wrote the inscription, how could she be certain of how she'd be buried?"

He'd seen where she was going with that. "But if she

already had a certain angel to which the amulet belonged…"

"Something on which she'd worked her magic," Anne had finished.

"Sounds whoo woo," he'd said with a grin.

"Very," she'd agreed. "But if we're lucky, that statue would have been donated to St. Theresa's along with the money."

And now, as they stood in the courtyard, he had to agree. It was filled with angel statues, some standing serenely, some with swords or trumpets. Some with wings spread. Some even appearing to fly.

"Hopefully, it's one of these."

One stood in the center of the courtyard on a pedestal surrounded by roses. "Look," Reg said, pointing to the statue. He heard Anne's intake of breath, and knew that she'd seen the same thing he did: an indentation within the stone breast of the statue just big enough to hold the amulet.

He met her eyes, and she nodded. Slowly, reverently, he moved toward the statue, then placed the amulet back into the breast of the angel.

There were no fireworks, no flares, no marching band.

But it was over.

He stepped back and found Anne beside him. Without a word, he pulled her close, sliding his mouth over hers. She opened for him, a soft moan escaping as she curled her arms around him. He slid his hands over her back possessively, wanting her desperately, and knowing he had her. She was his now, truly. Everything about her told him so, the way she pressed against him, the way she kissed him, the way her heart beat hard against his chest.

"Anne," he murmured. "Dear God, I love you."

She stroked his cheek, her smile gentle. "Can you tell if it's over?" she asked. "Did the earth move?"

He laughed, then kissed her again, hard. "It just did, sweetheart. It just did."

Epilogue

IT WAS THE FIRST TIME in too many years that Reg had not dreaded the coming of April 1. He was looking forward to it with anticipation, excitement. Triumph.

Finally, he'd beaten the curse.

The alarm in his watch beeped, signaling midnight. The start of a new era, the start of the rest of their lives. They were so lucky. Really.

From outside the bedroom window of the Dawes ancestral home, the gas lamps of New Orleans glowed warm and familiar. Inside, candles flickered, shadows dancing on the high ceilings and the velvet-covered walls. Reg looked over at his wife with loving eyes, knowing he'd found something better, as well.

Anne.

The bedroom was cluttered with boxes still waiting to be unpacked, but there had been other things, more important things to take care of when they arrived yesterday. Namely, making love to his wife. A man had to have his priorities.

Her lashes fluttered open, and he felt the familiar tightening in his heart. One year they'd been together as a couple, and the reaction never changed. She smiled and reached out a hand to stroke his cheek, and Reg felt another tightening. Lower, but no less important, and once again, Reg reordered his priorities.

Before he could react as biology dictated he should, his phone vibrated, and he read the text message. Frowned.

"What's wrong?" Anne asked.

"Nothing," he reassured her, still sounding confident because this wasn't a big deal. An annoyance, a mere neurological gnat.

The phone vibrated again. Another incoming message, this one from Darcy.

Impossible. Anne looked at him, worry in her face. "Is everything all right?"

"Everything's fine," he said with a laugh, a little less confident. A sinking pit low in his stomach replaced the very nice and completely ignorant bliss that had been there earlier.

The phone vibrated again, and as Reg read Devon's words, the full impact sunk in. They hadn't broken the curse.

Oops.

"I might have miscalculated," he began.

"You don't miscalculate," she cut in, still defending him. Still completely sure of him.

"This time, I might have," he stated, to keep the record straight.

"How so?"

"I should have made sure. I should have tested this out. But I didn't. It's not over. And now you're stuck."

She arched a graceful, yet militant brow. "Stuck?"

Not surprisingly, she didn't look unhappy, nor comfortable nor, as he'd so cleverly put it, "stuck." But Anne had never been the one with doubts. That'd been Reg. "Not stuck. If you want to leave, I'll understand."

That was a complete lie, but Reg chose not to muddy the waters with pesky things such as emotion and panic and the complete destruction of all happiness as he'd come to know it.

"What if I don't want to leave? What if I'm happy right where I am?"

And once again, his lungs began to function as before. "Certainly that's what you've always told me. But things aren't quite as easy as before. You had expectations of calm. Of goodness."

"Reg," she started, in a bossy voice that got him hard all over again.

"What?"

Her hands twined around his neck, into his hair, tangling there as if she meant to keep him. "I loved you before the calm, before the goodness. It doesn't matter to me. I love you."

"I know that," he insisted.

"For better, for worse," she insisted, right back at him. Stubborn as always, which was one of the main reasons he loved her.

"Jenna's having her baby in a cab somewhere on the George Washington Bridge," he said, trying to make her understand what "worse" actually entailed.

"She's a doctor. I'm sure she'll know what to do."

"Devon's house got destroyed once again."

"That's why she works for an insurance company."

"And Darcy's stranded on Cape Cod with Evan."

"And I'm sure she's happy as a clam because of it."

"It doesn't bother you?"

"I've got you. Nothing's going to bother me."

And finally, his heart began to ease. Not that he'd doubted her at all.

Reg leaned down, and as his mouth covered hers, a cold breeze blew through the house, overturning the candle and setting the chenille blanket on fire.

Calmly, Anne beat out the flame, one-handed, not even pausing in mid-kiss.

Cursed? Not a chance, Reg scoffed. Not a chance.

* * * * *

*Harlequin Intrigue top author Delores Fossen
presents a brand-new series of
breathtaking romantic suspense!*
TEXAS MATERNITY: HOSTAGES
The first installment available May 2010:
THE BABY'S GUARDIAN

Shaw cursed and hooked his arm around Sabrina.

Despite the urgency that the deadly gunfire created, he tried to be careful with her, and he took the brunt of the fall when he pulled her to the ground. His shoulder hit hard, but he held on tight to his gun so that it wouldn't be jarred from his hand.

Shaw didn't stop there. He crawled over Sabrina, sheltering her pregnant belly with his body, and he came up ready to return fire.

This was obviously a situation he'd wanted to avoid at all cost. He didn't want his baby in the middle of a fight with these armed fugitives, but when they fired that shot, they'd left him no choice. Now, the trick was to get Sabrina safely out of there.

"Get down," someone on the SWAT team yelled from the roof of the adjacent building.

Shaw did. He dropped lower, covering Sabrina as best he could.

There was another shot, but this one came from a rifleman on the SWAT team. Shaw didn't look up, but he heard the sound of glass being blown apart.

The shots continued, all coming from his men, which meant it might be time to try to get Sabrina to better cover. Shaw glanced at the front of the building.

So that Sabrina's pregnant belly wouldn't be smashed against the ground, Shaw eased off her and moved her to a sitting position so that her back was against the brick wall. They were close. Too close. And face-to-face.

He found himself staring right into those sea-green eyes.

How will Shaw get Sabrina out?
Follow the daring rescue and the heartbreaking
aftermath in THE BABY'S GUARDIAN
by Delores Fossen,
available May 2010 from Harlequin Intrigue.

HARLEQUIN® *Blaze*™

is proud to introduce...

New York Times bestselling author

Brenda Jackson

with
SPONTANEOUS

Kim Cannon and Duan Jeffries have a great thing going.
Whenever they meet up, the passion between them
is hot, intense…spontaneous. And things really heat
up when Duan agrees to accompany her to her
mother's wedding. Too bad there's something
he's not telling her.…

Don't miss the fireworks!

*Available in May 2010
wherever Harlequin Blaze books are sold.*

red-hot reads

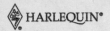

REQUEST YOUR FREE BOOKS!

2 FREE NOVELS
PLUS 2
FREE GIFTS!

HARLEQUIN®

Blaze™

Red-hot reads!

YES! Please send me 2 FREE Harlequin® Blaze™ novels and my 2 FREE gifts (gifts are worth about $10). After receiving them, if I don't wish to receive any more books, I can return the shipping statement marked "cancel." If I don't cancel, I will receive 6 brand-new novels every month and be billed just $4.24 per book in the U.S. or $4.71 per book in Canada. That's a saving of at least 15% off the cover price. It's quite a bargain. Shipping and handling is just 50¢ per book.* I understand that accepting the 2 free books and gifts places me under no obligation to buy anything. I can always return a shipment and cancel at any time. Even if I never buy another book, the two free books and gifts are mine to keep forever.

151/351 HDN E5LS

Name _____ (PLEASE PRINT)

Address _____ Apt. #

City _____ State/Prov. _____ Zip/Postal Code

Signature (if under 18, a parent or guardian must sign)

Mail to the **Harlequin Reader Service:**
IN U.S.A.: P.O. Box 1867, Buffalo, NY 14240-1867
IN CANADA: P.O. Box 609, Fort Erie, Ontario L2A 5X3

Not valid for current subscribers to Harlequin Blaze books.

Want to try two free books from another line?
Call 1-800-873-8635 or visit www.morefreebooks.com.

* Terms and prices subject to change without notice. Prices do not include applicable taxes. N.Y. residents add applicable sales tax. Canadian residents will be charged applicable provincial taxes and GST. Offer not valid in Quebec. This offer is limited to one order per household. All orders subject to approval. Credit or debit balances in a customer's account(s) may be offset by any other outstanding balance owed by or to the customer. Please allow 4 to 6 weeks for delivery. Offer available while quantities last.

Your Privacy: Harlequin Books is committed to protecting your privacy. Our Privacy Policy is available online at www.eHarlequin.com or upon request from the Reader Service. From time to time we make our lists of customers available to reputable third parties who may have a product or service of interest to you. If you would prefer we not share your name and address, please check here. ☐

Help us get it right—We strive for accurate, respectful and relevant communications. To clarify or modify your communication preferences, visit us at www.ReaderService.com/consumerschoice.

HB10R

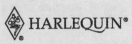

HARLEQUIN®

LAURA MARIE ALTOM

The Baby Twins

Stephanie Olmstead has her hands full raising
her twin baby girls on her own. When she runs
into old friend Brady Flynn, she's shocked to find
herself suddenly attracted to the handsome airline
pilot! Will this flyboy be the perfect daddy—
or will he crash and burn?

"LOVE, HOME & HAPPINESS"